Boy's Own
COMPANION No. 4

Edited by

JACK COX

Editor of Boy's Own Paper

LUTTERWORTH PRESS
LONDON

Printed in Great Britain by Cox and Wyman Limited
London, Reading and Fakenham

THE EDITOR'S PAGE

Boy's Own Companion is now an annual publication, and the many letters and comments we receive from *B.O.P* readers and their friends show that it is appreciated and anticipated every year in good time for Christmas. This is the fourth volume, and we hope very much that it will find a welcome place on your bookshelves alongside *Nos. 1, 2,* and *3*. If you are a new reader of *Boy's Own Paper* and, perhaps, seeing the *Companion* for the first time, we hasten to tell you that you can still buy copies of the first three volumes through your local bookseller, but if there is any difficulty then do write to us and we can help you to obtain copies.

Once again we present an edited collection of some of the best contributions to *B.O.P* since 1946, when I became Editor. Heading the list of contributors who have written stories is the world-famous Hammond Innes, a genuine *B.O.P* enthusiast. At various times he has written serials, stories, and articles about sailing for us; sometimes they have been written in his home in a Suffolk village and sometimes on board his magnificent ocean-going yacht, as in this case. *Voyage Into Danger* is really three stories taken from the log of the yacht *Dorothea*, and I know you will like them. Group Captain S. C. George, who now lives in Hampshire after many years' service in Australia, Malaya and elsewhere, is the author of *Buffalo Country*, and H. B. Gregory, a young Birmingham author, writes an intriguing space story entitled *Runaway Rocket*.

One of America's best-known authors and humorists, B. J. Chute, who had the good fortune to have one American and one English parent, shows the problems that photographers face in *Camera Shy*. A British playwright, Colin Robertson, who is a Yorkshireman now living in North London, also well known as an adult thriller writer, is the author of a splendid one-act play *Out of the Night*. It is just right for that show you are planning in the new church hall or your youth club.

What else can we offer you? Patrick Moore, the B.B.C. Television astronomer, discusses something very topical in *Signals From Outer Space*, and Edward Pyddoke, of the London Institute of Archaeology, shows how *Photos Help the Archaeologist*. P. W. Blandford describes in detail how to make the *B.O.P* Dinghy and adds lots of first-rate advice on sailing (complete, full size plans can be obtained from the author c/o *B.O.P*). You can also search for beach jewels with Trevor Holloway, collect cheese labels, make masks for fun or decoration, or designs from your own camera, or build some fascinating indoor flying models with the expert R. H. Warring, a most popular and very talented contributor to the magazine. Practical boys will also find plenty of activity in making Gilbert Davey's one-valve radio receiver or in setting up the Boy's Own Workshop.

How do birds navigate? No one knows for certain but Richard Fitter tells you as much as modern scientists know, and a really interesting story it is, too. Another naturalist in L. Hugh Newman, of our *Nature Can be Fun* page, shows boys how to set up a Nature Den, while C. F. Snow, our expert on rabbits, cavies, hamsters and mice, advises on the art of keeping rabbits in colonies.

Jeff Jeffries, who joined the *B.O.P* team recently, has already made many friends with his "True Life Adventure" stories of the early days of the United States. One of them on *Wyatt Earp—Fighting Marshal* is included in this *Companion*. Then there's the new sport of karting, as well as keeping budgerigars for pleasure and profit, setting up a dark room, and "beating the bounds" of your town or county on a bike; if you are a jazz fan you will certainly enjoy Rex Harris's entertaining story about The Temperance Seven.

The *B.O.P* team and the *B.O.P* staff join me once more in sending you good wishes and greetings wherever you may be, for we know our readers live in all parts of the world—in fact, in 55 countries at the present time. We thank you for all your kind letters and constructive comments which have helped in no small way to shape the contents of this *Boy's Own Companion*. I shall always be glad to hear from any reader, and to do my best to help you if you have a problem or query.

JACK COX,
4 BOUVERIE STREET,
LONDON,
E.C.4.

CONTENTS

Sport

Outdoor Life

Hobbies

Detection

Humour and Verse

Miscellaneous

ACKNOWLEDGEMENTS

The publishers wish to thank the following copyright holders for permission to reproduce the photographs in this book: Messrs. French Line (Plate 1); Raymond Cripps (Plate 2); Centraal Fotopersbureau, Rotterdam (Plate 3b); Messrs. Curtiss-Wright Inc., U.S.A. (Plate 3a); Messrs. Trokart Manufacturing Company, Croydon (Plate 4a); G. E. Harris (Plate 4b); D. H. Hillesley (Plate 5); Society of Antiquaries (Plate 6a), and George L. Wakefield (Plate 7).

LIST OF PLATES

VOYAGE INTO DANGER

by

HAMMOND INNES

THE LAST TRIP

IT was early November, the air still, almost balmy. A weather-breeder, I thought, as I rowed out from Customs Pier, for there were wisps of cloud streamered across the sky. The *Dorothea* was a big boat. She'd be quite a handful for three men if it blew up dirty. But it didn't worry me until I was close alongside and saw the mass of ropes that formed her rigging. They were mostly new ropes, which was odd considering it was the end of the season and she was going over to France to be sold: new ropes, stiff and hard to handle, and not a winch in the whole ship, everything done by purchases running through dozens of blocks.

Then I was on board, being welcomed by Dr. Fenton, and I found myself hoping that the third member of the crew, whom he'd called Peter, would be a youngster with plenty of muscle, for I was shocked at the change in him. It was three or four years since we'd last met and I remembered him as a distinguished-looking, very vital man, regarded as one of the country's leading brain specialists. That had been at Cowes and he'd been racing his own six-metre yacht. Now he seemed shrunken and aged, his hair white and the skin of his face stretched taut across the bone. But the eyes were the same, amazingly blue and almost hypnotic in their intensity. He took me below and there was a girl in the big mahogany-panelled saloon. He introduced her to me as his daughter and I asked her whether she was coming with us, for she was dressed for sea in blue serge trousers and sweater.

"Of course Peter is coming with us," the doctor said.

Peter! Great Scott! This was the stalwart lad I had expected as the third member of the crew. An old man and a girl—it was impossible! But when I started to tell him so, the doctor became violently excited. He refused to listen to my reasons, reminding me that I was being paid for the job, that I was a professional deliverer of yachts, and that he intended putting to sea right away. "I'll get the engine started while you stow your gear."

I began to follow him up on to the deck, but a hand touched my arm. "Please." It was the girl. "Don't excite him. And don't let him down.

13

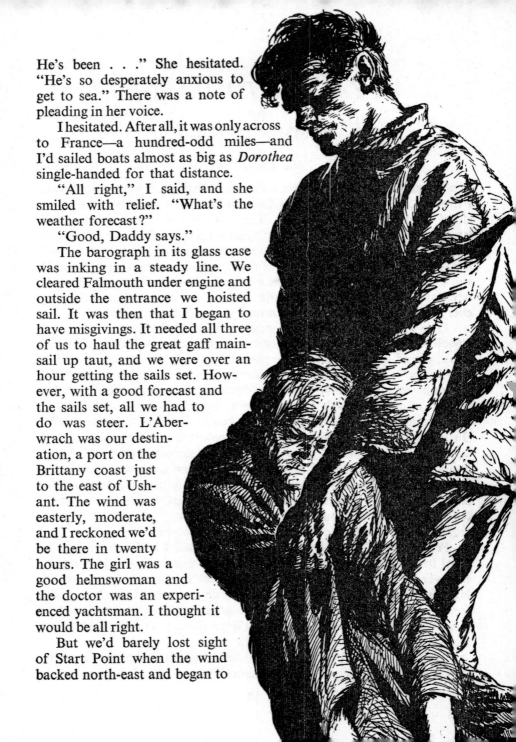

He's been . . ." She hesitated. "He's so desperately anxious to get to sea." There was a note of pleading in her voice.

I hesitated. After all, it was only across to France—a hundred-odd miles—and I'd sailed boats almost as big as *Dorothea* single-handed for that distance.

"All right," I said, and she smiled with relief. "What's the weather forecast?"

"Good, Daddy says."

The barograph in its glass case was inking in a steady line. We cleared Falmouth under engine and outside the entrance we hoisted sail. It was then that I began to have misgivings. It needed all three of us to haul the great gaff mainsail up taut, and we were over an hour getting the sails set. However, with a good forecast and the sails set, all we had to do was steer. L'Aberwrach was our destination, a port on the Brittany coast just to the east of Ushant. The wind was easterly, moderate, and I reckoned we'd be there in twenty hours. The girl was a good helmswoman and the doctor was an experienced yachtsman. I thought it would be all right.

But we'd barely lost sight of Start Point when the wind backed north-east and began to blow. Night was coming on and we'd have to shorten sail. "What was that forecast?" I asked the doctor. "You told your daughter it was good."

"It was all right!" he murmured and his eyes slid away from me. There was something queer about the man, almost crafty, as he shambled away into his cabin aft. I checked the barograph then. It hadn't been wound up. The needle was stationary and I'd been too busy on deck to get the six-o'clock forecast. I went up to the cockpit where the girl was at the wheel, and asked her straight out whether she'd known the forecast was bad, and she nodded unhappily.

"You didn't like it when you found the third member of the crew was a girl, did you?" she said.

"What's that got to do with it?"

"Daddy was afraid if we waited you'd refuse to come with us."

So that was it. But it was a crazy thing to do and I told her so, and her eyes widened with the shock of my words. She loved her father and whatever he did, it seemed, was right as far as she was concerned.

"Why does he call you Peter?"

She smiled then. "Medical psychology. I was supposed to be a boy!"

We shortened sail and, as though to make amends, the doctor worked hard. After that he took the wheel while Peter got a meal. I had decided that it was better to go on than turn and beat back against the wind. The forecast at 11.50 was wind north-east, fresh to strong. The sea wasn't too bad and we would be in L'Aber-wrach by midday. L'Aberwrach! It was not L'Aberwrach the doctor was headed for. When he relieved me in the grey light of dawn he told me the real destination. It was the Azores. They would pick up the trade winds there and sail the boat across to America. For a moment I thought he was joking, and then all the things that had puzzled me fell into place—the new rigging, the mass of charts, the lockers crammed with stores, and words overheard just after we'd sailed from Falmouth: "Think of it, Peter— we've started. A new world. A world where new ideas aren't crushed out of a man by stupidity, and experiments can be carried on . . ." He meant it.

"You must be mad," I said. "We'd be exhausted before we got half-way across the Bay of Biscay."

15

He offered me money. He pleaded with me. In the end I left him sitting hunched over the wheel. I'd take him to L'Aberwrach and that was all. I told the girl to put her foot down. "He'll kill himself, and you, too. It's crazy."

But all she said was, "I can't let him down now. He needs this—this escape." Her voice sounded strangely tired. "He's happier at sea."

Visibility was fair and we should have sighted the coast at ten o'clock. But by midday there was still no sign of land. One o'clock . . . two, and still no land. For the third time I checked my navigation. We had come a hundred and twenty miles by the log since Start Point. On the course we had been steering we should have been in L'Aberwrach two hours ago. It was then that I began to feel scared, for the wind was blowing gale force in the gusts and the seas were huge. A dirty cloud wrack filled the sky. Ushant weather!

Ushant! I guessed what was wrong then, and was shocked when I discovered the cause. A piece of metal had been placed close against the compass. The needle had been deflected and, instead of steering for L'Aberwrach, we had headed farther west and were out in the Atlantic beyond Ushant. When I confronted the doctor with this, he only smiled and shrugged his shoulders. "Now you'll have to come with us," he said.

"You crazy fool!" I shouted. "Don't you realize there's a gale coming up?"

But it didn't seem to register and a chill crept over me. The man was mad—mad in the sense that he was beyond all reason or sense of responsibility, obsessed with an idea. "He ought to be locked up," I told his daughter.

She looked at me and said. "Perhaps. But this was his release, his escape. I couldn't face the other. It would have finished him. I'm sorry."

We couldn't turn back. The seas were too big. We ran before it under reefed main and storm jib. The wind rose to a shrieking crescendo and the sea turned to white as the wind drove the spindrift from the breaking waves. Night closed in and the sails were still set. I should have had them down and been running under bare poles, but I'd left it too late. The doctor was seasick by then.

"Never suffered from it before," he groaned at me from his bunk, his face green and haggard and wet with sweat. Just the girl and I and the ship thundering through the night with white water seething across the cockpit. Soon she couldn't hold the wheel any longer, and I sent her

16

below and lashed myself into the cockpit. I remember the dawn and another night and the sails blowing themselves to ribbons. After that we streamed warps to keep her stern to the waves. The hatch was smashed in and I nailed a sail over the gaping hole. But water still came in and we pumped till we collapsed exhausted, and when the water was up to the bunks we pumped again.

*　　　*　　　*

It was the pumping that killed Dr. Fenton. He gave to it his last reserves of energy, and when he collapsed I put him in his bunk, and the girl and I went on pumping. We only discovered he was dead after the steamer had sighted us and was lying up-wind of us, pumping oil on to the water. She was a big freighter and she came down on us, rolling heavily, with rope ladders over her side, and we just got clear of *Dorothea* before the mast went and all her starboard side was stove in against the iron hull. From the heaving deck of the steamer I watched as *Dorothea* sank slowly and I hated to see her go. It was so unnecessary. In some way I felt responsible and because of this I wanted to find out all I could about her. The two stories that follow are reproduced as far as possible in the words in which they were told to me.

A RESPECTABLE YACHTSMAN ADVERTISES

ACCORDING to the Certificate of Registry, *Dorothea*'s previous owner had been Colonel James Ellison. He had purchased her from Admiralty Disposals late in 1947. He sailed her all the following season, going foreign several times, but never farther than the north coast of France. He belonged to several yacht clubs, kept the boat at Cowes, and raced her twice. In the autumn he had the following advertisement inserted in one of the yachting magazines:

Young man wanted to complete crew of Bristol Channel pilot cutter yacht cruising Mediterranean this winter. Must be personable, have reasonable experience and be free for minimum of three months. All expenses paid. Box No. 6574.

Among the young men who answered that advertisement was Bill Lytton, 27 years old. The rest is best told in his own words. . . .

I met Colonel Ellison by arrangement at his London club (he said) and a fortnight later I joined *Dorothea* at Dover. She was lying in

Wellington Dock with a film of coal dust on her deck and I found the ship's company down below waiting for the weather forecast. There was a Commander, Pat Fairbrother, and a paid hand called Mike, who had been a stoker in the Navy. The ship was all ready to put to sea, but it was blowing a gale out in the Channel. Later on I went ashore.

A man stood in the shadows by the boatyard slipway. From where he stood he looked across to *Dorothea*'s deck. When I had passed him I heard the man's footsteps on the gravel behind me. He quickened his pace and caught up with me.

"You're from the yacht *Dorothea*, aren't you?"

"Yes," I said. "Why?"

"I'm a police officer. I'm going to take a chance," he said, suddenly. "I'd say you were straight, and if you're straight you'll do as I ask."

What he wanted me to do was to tip him off a few hours before Colonel Ellison sailed. "He won't be sailing tonight because of the gale," he said. "But tomorrow . . ." He hesitated. "The trouble is," he added, "I can't arrest him until he's actually sailed, and I need time to organize a launch."

"What's he supposed to have done?" I asked. But he wouldn't tell me that, and in the end I agreed to do what he asked. I walked for over an hour after that. In the end I decided that the only honest thing to do was to tell Ellison what had happened.

He took it calmly without any show of surprise. "So he doesn't think we'd sail tonight." He turned to the Commander. "What time do the dock gates open tonight, Pat?"

18

"Two-thirty. But the gale!" the Commander said.

"Forget the gale! It won't be the last we'll have before we reach Tangier."

It was the first I'd heard of our going to Tangier and I told him I wasn't sailing unless I knew what it was all about.

"All right, Bill," he said, "I'll tell you."

He explained then that he'd been trying to get his money out of the country legally ever since the war. "But they wouldn't let me, so I began buying diamonds. Every penny I possess is invested in diamonds and they're all here on board."

There was nothing illegal in a man possessing diamonds. It was only illegal when he tried to take them out of the country without an export licence. That's why they couldn't do anything about it until he sailed. It took me a little time to work out my attitude to this. But, after all, it was his own money. Morally he hadn't done anything wrong, and at that time I was getting sick of regulations myself. In the end I agreed to go with him and at two-thirty we started the engine, slipped the warps and motored quietly out of the dock, past the lights of the Channel packet.

The wind had eased a bit but it was still blowing Force 6 or 7 from the south-east, and in the comparatively quiet water of the outer harbour we hoisted reefed main and storm jib. The western entrance of Dover Harbour was still closed with block ships in those days, and all traffic had to use the eastern entrance. As we approached it the signal lights turned against us, and while we were jogging back and forth, waiting for a cross-Channel steamer, a big motor-boat came out from the submarine base.

The lights changed and we went steaming through the gap between the stone buttresses of the breakwater. Once outside, our whole attention was concentrated on sailing, for the tide off the eastern entrance whips up an ugly sea in a gale. It wasn't until we were several miles off Dover, with the harbour lights already blurred, that I noticed the motor-boat following us. Ellison had seen it, too, for he had us alter course to the south-west and then we hoisted the staysail and took one roll out of the mainsail reefing.

We were heeled right over then, tearing along at eight knots with the lee deck half buried in water. But the motor-boat had followed our change of course and was still coming up on us, her white mast-head light swaying wildly as she rolled in the heavy seas. Ellison stood and watched her for a time, his bulky, oilskin-clad figure balanced to the

19

swoop and pitch of the deck. Then he dived into the charthouse and I saw him poring over the chart and out ahead of us a light winked in the darkness.

*   *   *

When he came out he spoke to the Commander, who was at the wheel. I heard the word "Varne" mentioned, and the Commander said, "Don't be a fool, Jimmy."

"There's just enough water," Ellison answered. "They'll never dare follow us through those seas."

The Varne is a shallow bank in mid-Channel and it was the Varne buoy that was winking at us out ahead. We passed it quite close and altered course to the west. Half an hour later we were crossing the bank. The sea turned to white; great combers reared up and broke, crashing down on to the deck and showering us with pebble scooped up from the sea bed only a few feet below our keel.

Then we struck. The shock of it flung me off my feet. A breaker rose up, curled and broke with a great roar of water. The ship staggered under the weight of sea and wind, shook herself free, struck again and then went rolling on. We were across, in deep water, and no sign of the motor-boat. But Mike had broken his leg. Later there was water over the floorboards of the saloon, and we began to pump. There was nothing for it but to make port as quickly as possible. The wind was veering to the south. France was out of the question. It had to be England.

We limped into Folkestone at dawn and got Mike to hospital while the boatyard people pumped *Dorothea* out and hauled her up on to the slip. Nobody came to arrest Ellison. The police took no interest in us at all. Even when I returned to my old address in London they didn't come to question me; nor did they question Ellison.

I didn't discover the answer until about a year later. I picked up a paper and saw a picture of the man who had stopped me in Dover and told me he was a police officer. It was taken against the background of a big motor-boat. He was described as a smuggler and he had been arrested at Gibraltar following a running gun battle at sea with a Tangier boat. We had never been chased by a police boat. The man had known about the diamonds and he'd used me as a means of frightening Ellison into putting to sea. On a night like that he could have got away with murder, even in the crowded waters of the Dover Straits. Looking back on it, it was all rather amusing. But it wasn't so amusing at the time.

AGROUND ON LONG SAND HEAD

AT the time of the Munich Crisis in 1938, *Dorothea* was involved in a rather curious affair. Unfortunately, I have not been able to find any one person who could tell the whole story and I have, therefore, strung the facts together as best I can from statements made by the people concerned. At that time *Dorothea* had already been converted to a yacht. Early in September her owner brought her up to Pin Mill on the Orwell estuary, which runs down from Ipswich to Harwich, and left her in charge of the boatyard. A few nights later she disappeared from her moorings.

The boatyard contacted the owner and then reported her loss to the police. Shipping was asked to look out for her, but the search was hampered by thick fog, which did not clear until the evening. The following morning Trinity House depot received a radio message from the master of one of the ships serving the light vessels of the Thames Estuary.

"Proceeding from the Kentish Knock towards the Shipwash light vessel at 0520 hours I failed to observe the flashes of the Long Sand Head buoy. I altered course to investigate and found the light obstructed by a man clinging to the buoy. I lowered a boat and took him off. He had been there since the afternoon of the previous day, having been stranded there from the yacht *Dorothea*.

"His name is John Price and he is a Cambridge undergraduate. He has no knowledge of destination or present whereabouts of yacht. Have not questioned him further as he is suffering from exposure. The severed end of a heavy warp was found attached to the buoy."

When the Trinity House ship returned to Harwich shortly after midday, Price was taken to the police station, where he was charged with being implicated in stealing the yacht *Dorothea*. He then made a statement:

"We boarded the yacht about midnight and set sail. There was four of us altogether. Everything went smoothly until we got out beyond the Cork Light vessel. Then the fog came down. There wasn't much wind and we drifted about till dawn. Some time during the night we hit a buoy. I think it marked the bottom of the Shipwash.

"By morning I wasn't sure where we were. There were ships all around us. We could hear their foghorns, and once we were almost run down—a big passenger steamer that passed so close we could almost touch her sides. Then the wind got up and the sea with it. We were in six fathoms and I was scared the tide was carrying us down on to a sand bank. I anchored and got the sails off.

"About an hour later the cable parted and we began to drift. Shortly afterwards a buoy came towards us out of the fog. It was Long Sand Head buoy and I decided to get a rope across to it and so save us from being carried on to the Long Sand. I dived overboard as the tide carried *Dorothea* past and made a rope fast to the iron cage of the buoy.

"Unfortunately the rope parted and the yacht disappeared into the fog, carried very rapidly by the tide and wind. It was about 3.30 then and I was clinging to the buoy until 5.30 this morning. I regret very much taking the boat. We never intended to when we rowed out to her. It was done for a lark on the spur of the moment. The others had never sailed before and they thought it would be fun to try."

23

He refused to give the names of his companions and was returned to his cell. At that point the police were satisfied that it was no more than a youthful escapade, and no further action would have been taken but for Lieutenant-Commander Slater, the Naval Intelligence Officer, who happened to be in the building at the time and saw the statement.

He was immediately struck by two things. The warp had parted before Price had had time to swim back to the yacht and yet the Master of the Trinity House vessel, whose statement he had already seen, had specifically described the severed end as that of a heavy warp. Also he failed to see how the yacht could have disappeared into the fog too quickly for Price to swim back to her. Once in the water he would have been carried along with the tide and, unless the sail had been hoisted, the wind could not have moved the yacht faster than he could swim.

Price was brought in again and questioned on these two points. Slater, in his final report on the affair, described Price as "confused and very frightened". In the end he had admitted that he'd severed the rope himself.

"Do you mean to say," Slater said, "that you deliberately cut the yacht adrift, knowing that you would be marooned on that buoy in a thick fog? But why?" Slater kept on battering at him on this point and finally he admitted that it was because he had become scared of his companions.

"Which one in particular?" Slater demanded.

"Murphy." The name slipped out automatically, but he wouldn't say why he'd been scared of him. Puzzled, Slater returned to his office. It was the fact that one of the men was Irish that worried him. The Irish Republican Army was becoming active again at that time.

In the end he rang Cambridge, checking on Price's background. He discovered that the boy was half-Irish and that during the vacation he'd had a part-time job at an electrical works in the district and had been friendly with a group of Irishmen. He telephoned the factory. Quickly they checked through their Irish employees. Three men— David Boyd, Patrick Murphy and Michael Finnigan—had failed to report for duty the day before. Moreover, an oxy-acetylene blow torch was missing.

Back at the police station he confronted Price with what he had discovered. Price broke down then. He admitted that his companions had had a portable blow torch with them. The idea had been to cut through the mooring chains of several yachts to give the police something to think about. But when they got out to *Dorothea* they'd insisted on

24

taking the boat to sea. It wasn't until he'd made the warp fast to the Long Sand Head buoy, and they'd told him to stay on it whilst one of them went down to examine the size of the buoy's securing cable, that he'd realized what the blow torch was really for. They were planning to cut adrift the buoys that marked the banks running up into the Thames Estuary.

He'd tried to make them understand that it would endanger the lives of a great many men, but Murphy had shouted at him that he'd kill him if he didn't shut up and do as he was told. That was when he'd severed the warp with his knife. It was what Slater had feared and he lost no time. Within a quarter of an hour he was steaming out of Harwich in a fast naval launch. It was already late in the day and if night fell before he'd discovered what buoys they'd cut adrift . . . it didn't bear thinking about.

He checked charts and tides as the launch ploughed eastwards through the Medusa Channel and fixed *Dorothea*'s position when the fog had lifted as six miles south-west of the Long Sand Head buoy, at the entrance to the Black Deep. Four miles to the north-west of her the vital Sunk Head buoy, marking the top of the Sunk Sand, would have been clearly visible. This was the buoy he headed for first and he found it drifting five miles out of position. A mile away from it *Dorothea* stood motionless in the sea with all her sails still set. She was hard aground on the very sandbank destined for the graveyard of some big ship!

SCIENCE NEWS

Parabolic Binoculars

The latest binoculars gather five times as much light as ordinary binoculars and thus give a better, clearer image, especially under poor lighting conditions. The performance of conventional binoculars is really limited by weight. Improved performance means larger size and more weight and a limit is reached at which they are no longer convenient, or practical, to handle. A new design replaces the two objective lenses, a major source of weight, with a parabolic reflector made of highly polished aluminium and fitted with a clear-glass cover. Focusing is by means of a knob in the centre of the cover glass, which actually adjusts a central reflector directing the light beams into a conventional pair of eye-pieces for viewing. The complete apparatus looks rather like a pair of light-weight binoculars cut off short, with a disc resembling a flashgun reflector attached to the front.

The Shrewd Banker

1955
JULY 11 MONDAY

1. A bank manager received a call just after the bank opened, purporting to be from a client named Henry Martin, who was sending along a friend, Stephen Spence, with a cheque for £400.

2. The manager checked that Henry Martin' account was good for the sum mentioned on th telephone, and found that payment would leav only a few pounds to the client's credit.

No. 22 913029
42791
London & Southern Bank Ltd
BRIDEGATE BRANCH
10th July 1955
Pay Stephen Spence, Esq.   or Order
£400
Four hundred pounds only.
Henry Martin
R12

5. The manager glanced at the cheque which appeared to be quite in order. As it had not been crossed it would certainly be paid in cash, provided the cheque had been endorsed by Mr. Spence. It had been endorsed correctly on the reverse side.

6. When he had inspected the cheque and appeare to find it all in order the manager rose. "I'll jus check the account, Mr. Spence, if you don't mind,' he said. "I shan't keep you more than a few minutes Please excuse me."

What had the shrewd banker noticed that aroused his suspicions

Mr. Martin's friend arrived shortly after twelve
'clock. "Come in, Mr. Spence," said the manager.
Mr. Martin 'phoned that you were catching a train
nd wanted me to cash a cheque."

4. "That's right," said Mr. Spence, presenting the
cheque. "Mr. Martin made it out just before he
'phoned you. It clinches a business deal before I catch
my train."

The manager 'phoned Mr. Martin's home from
nother office and learned that his client was abroad
nd that the place had been burgled. He then 'phoned
uperintendent Slade. "The signature appears genuine,
ut I'm suspicious."

8. When Slade arrived he recognized the visitor at
once as a well-known crook and master forger. "Well,
well, Fingers," he greeted the other, "you nearly did
it again! But you shouldn't have aroused the manager's
suspicions."

ll the necessary clues are given.   Solution on page 191

WYATT EARP —
FIGHTING MARSHAL

by

JEFF JEFFRIES

DURING eight short but hectic years Wyatt Berry Stapp Earp built himself a reputation for fearless law-enforcement that has become a legend throughout the Americas. And yet this lean six-footer, with the cool grey eyes and quiet manner, had no intention of becoming a peace officer when he came West with his parents in 1864.

Son of an Illinois lawyer, farmer, and Captain of Militia, Wyatt Earp was destined for the Law, and might well have become a small town lawyer but for two things: his insatiable taste for adventure, and his first sight of Kansas City at the height of its glory.

To the sixteen-year-old boy newly arrived from the East, Kansas City presented a picture of bustle and excitement such as he had never visualized. Buffalo hunters, freighters, Indian Fighters, Army Scouts, prospectors, cattlemen, cowboys, and a thousand other frontiersmen of every known trade and profession thronged the streets as they hurried about their business, or idled on the wooden sidewalks to hear the latest gossip of the frontier. Kansas City was the outfitting town for all points North and West: the jumping off place for high adventure.

"There's a fortune to be made in buffalo hides," came the voice of a bronzed plainsman who leaned his buckskin-clad arms on the muzzle of his cumbersome Sharpe's Fifty rifle.

"There's gold up there all right," a grizzle-haired prospector stated with conviction. "Gold, and silver too if I'm any judge. Can't wait to get back with the tools and victuals."

"The richest grazing land in America," a cattleman avowed. "The Texan boys are pourin' cattle into the railheads by the hundred thousand. All they have to do is drive them slow along the Chisholm Trail an' they fatten on the hoof."

For a few months Wyatt Earp stuck grimly to his studies, but eventually the glamour of the frontier won. He threw up his studies of the Law and drove a four-mule team for a freighter hauling urgently needed supplies to the railroad construction gangs.

In turn he became guard and hunter to a Government Survey Party; horse dealer; freighter; and buffalo hunter. Within five years he developed into an able, hardened Westerner.

But there was another side to life on the frontier. Every day saw brawls and fist fights between Northerner and Southerner, buffalo hunter and prospector, and six-gun duels were commonplace. The Texan cattlemen paid off their riders at the railhead towns, and everywhere the toughened, trail-weary cowboys gathered was sure to be the scene of broken heads and sudden senseless shooting. Wherever Western men congregated the talk was liable to turn to tales of feuds and gunfights, of the merits of swivel or fixed holsters, of fanning hammers or disconnecting triggers for faster gunplay.

With customary thoroughness the young Illinoian turned his attention to firearms, and decided to learn from the deadliest shot in the West—Wild Bill Hickok.

Wild Bill was ever ready to show off his shooting prowess to an admiring audience. Trick shooting was his pride—his favourite trick being to split a sixgun bullet in two against the edge of a coin at twenty

29

paces, or to drive a cork into a bottle at the same distance. He added plenty of sound sense from his vast experience.

"Always take your time, son," he cautioned his pupil. "It's the man who rushes things who loses. Never try any fancy shooting in a gun-fight—it may not come off, and there won't be a second chance."

With constant practice Wyatt Earp soon became a first-rate shot, and the speed of his draw caused raised eyebrows among the experts. But Wyatt wasn't content with mere efficiency with firearms. His keen, inquiring brain told him that it was the man behind the gun who mattered. He began to study his fellow men with the same intense concentration that he had applied to mastery of his sixgun.

"Wyatt never made a move until he had figured all the angles," his old friend Bat Masterson recounted. "Then he went right out and did it with complete confidence in his ability to see it through."

This was Wyatt Earp's secret. He possessed that rare combination: the ability to act with supreme efficiency, and the ability to think—and think fast.

"He was a bluffer, so I went right up to him," was all he said of the notorious Sergeant King, who had a six gun levelled at him when they met in Witchita. It was left to others to describe how Wyatt snatched the gun from the would-be killer's hand, slapped his face, and marched him off to jail for disturbing the peace!

*   *   *

It was in Ellsworth, Kansas, that the frontier was to see the first appearance of the mature Wyatt Earp, and it was here that Fate took a hand in deciding his future for him.

Within hours of arriving at the bustling uproarious cattle town he saw the Sheriff killed by Bill Thompson, and the whole town held at bay by Ben Thompson's shotgun while brother Bill made good his escape.

The Town Marshal and his deputies refused to move when ordered to arrest the man—particularly when they saw a hundred Texan cowboys siding with the killer and openly defying the peace officers to "come out an' get us!"

"It's none of my business," Wyatt Earp said casually within earshot of the Mayor. "But if it was I'd get a gun and go out and arrest Ben Thompson myself."

"I'll make it your business!" came the unexpected reply; and before he quite knew what was happening the lean, serious-faced twenty-five-year-old found himself choosing a pair of sixguns at a nearby store and preparing to fulfil his boast before the entire population of Ellsworth.

Quite how he did it, or quite why he did it, Wyatt Earp never really knew. He just walked out into the open plaza with his borrowed guns still holstered, and ordered Ben Thompson to throw down his gun.

News of this single-handed feat ran through the prairie lands and cattle camps like wildfire, and soon the Mayors of neighbouring townships, desperately worried, were pleading with him to take over the job of law enforcement for them. Within weeks Wyatt Earp was made Marshal of Witchita.

He didn't waste any time. "No guns to be worn in Town", were his orders. It needed only the sight of a sixgun hanging at a cowboy's hip for the Marshal to whip out his Colt Peacemaker and hustle the protesting offender to the courthouse.

No matter what the offence, Wyatt Earp dealt with it promptly and appropriately. He didn't hide behind the security of his gun, and he didn't shoot unless he had no option. If a brawling bully needed taming he unbuckled his gunbelt and waded in with bare fists to give a lesson that would long be remembered.

Again the thinking Marshal had found the answer. Convinced that the scorn of their fellow cowboys was more deadly than gunplay, he developed his own technique of "buffaloing" lawbreakers. This consisted of snatching his Colt so fast that he could hit a man over the head with the barrel and knock him senseless before the other could fire. It took iron nerve and incredible speed, but Wyatt had them both.

The cattle kings bitterly resented the way they and their men were treated. A reward was offered secretly—1000 dollars to be paid to the man who ran the fighting Marshal out of town.

A dozen and more men tried for the reward. Wyatt met them all—man to man. Without exception they left town humiliated; beaten to the draw before their guns were half-out of their holsters.

Appointed Marshal of Dodge City, Wyatt Earp saw a continual run of such episodes. He faced the classic showdown with the ace gunfighter Clay Allison. He faced rough and tumbles, mass attacks, ambushes, and every kind of retaliation that men could devise. Wyatt survived them all—and Dodge City was tamed.

He died in 1928 at 80, a wealthy man with mining and oil interests in several States. A grateful Government named the little settlement of Earp, Colorado as a permanent memorial to the greatest Marshal of them all, Wyatt Earp, The Fighting Marshal.

HOW TO SET UP A NATURE DEN

by

L. HUGH NEWMAN

HAVE you ever felt the urge to collect something? It is usually very strongly developed among boys interested in the many aspects of wild life. But fashions change. Once men used to seek trophies in the tropics, mostly in the form of stuffed heads of the animals they killed, but we now prefer to "shoot" wild creatures with a ciné camera or collect ordinary photographs taken in their natural haunts.

Few of us can ever hope to go on safari to Africa or India, still the great centres of big game; but we can have any amount of fun and often much excitement, too, exploring our own countryside and collecting specimens as we go. It is better to be a specialist than just to go round haphazardly picking up this and that. Decide what interests you most and stick to it.

As a boy I had a craze for collecting birds' feathers. I made quite an imposing album by attaching them with cotton thread to sheets of clean blotting paper and then binding them all into a kind of loose-leaf folder. Now, when I turn its pages to show my own sons, each feather is a kind of talisman which, the moment I see it, recalls to my mind all the happy hours I spent searching for it in out-of-the-way places. Today I would probably mount feathers with "Sellotape" and make a far neater job of the whole thing, but the *fun* of making the collection would be just the same.

Planning a nature den is fun. I am sure many of you must have an old garden shed or an attic room which you could easily convert into a "bug room". I know a school Natural History Society which was given just such a place to convert into a school museum. The first thing to do is to make your "den" as light as possible, especially if you want to try and breed insects there. You can probably get permission to paint the walls with one of the gay emulsion paints, using a light and cheerful colour. You will be surprised what a difference it will make. We recently had our Scout clubroom painted primrose yellow; it was extremely effective and much lighter and more cheerful than the familiar old brown paint.

You will need a work table of some kind and the best position for this is under the window where you get the light you need for mounting your specimens, whether they be butterflies and moths, beetles, flies, or any other small creatures. If you cannot make a table yourself you may be able to get one cheaply at a local auction sale. In a very small room it might be a good idea to have a "flap" table hinged to the wall, so that you can let it down to make more space when you are not actually working at it.

To make the most of your room you should fix up plenty of shelves to hold books, apparatus, and specimens. Do see that they are reasonably wide, at least 12 inches I should say, so that cages and boxes and pots can stand on them without danger of toppling off. Take care to fix the brackets securely and screw the shelves firmly to the brackets. I remember the day when a shelf gave way in one of my breeding rooms on my Butterfly Farm in Kent; down came all the glass cylinders and cages smashed to pieces on the floor; much valuable livestock was destroyed.

A strong cupboard with well-fitting doors is a very useful thing to have; again you could probably pick one up so cheaply at some local sale that it would hardly be worth your while to make one, even if you are a handyman. It will probably want stripping down and repainting, but when the job is done you will have somewhere to keep your microscope, setting boards, entomological pins, forceps, scalpels, and all the other odds and ends needed by a working naturalist.

Breeding Insects

If you go in for breeding insects you will need plenty of cages but they need not be elaborate. Wooden boxes can be easily converted into breeding cages by cutting "windows" in the sides and covering them with gauze or netting to allow plenty of fresh air to enter. Even ordinary large shoe boxes are excellent and you can probably get a good supply of these from your local shoe shop. Cut a square out of the centre of each lid, leaving a margin about an inch wide all round the edge. Now buy some cheap curtain netting and cut it into pieces a little larger than the boxes. Drape the netting over the open box, slip the lid back into place and you have a breeding cage all ready to use, after fixing the lid with a couple of rubber bands. Standing on end these boxes make excellent cages for small numbers of feeding caterpillars and will easily hold a small jar or bottle of food plant. In the normal position you can use them as emerging cages for butterflies and moths or as laying cages for any female moths you may have caught or bred.

Another useful kind of cage for all sorts of insects is a flower pot. You can either cover it with a sheet of glass, or if you want to make it larger, rig up a framework of wire hoops and drape netting or gauze over this. If the pot is large enough you could even induce butterflies to lay in a cage like this, if you provided them with flowers and the right kind of food plant, if possible actually growing in the pot.

If you breed or catch insects your specimens must be properly mounted. Butterflies and moths are set on boards with their wings spread out and allowed to remain there for about a month, until they are quite dry. It is not easy to set well, but you will master it in time if you practise. If possible ask somebody who knows to show you the correct method. Insects of all kinds will quickly deteriorate unless you store them away in air-tight boxes where moths and mites cannot attack them. Entomological store boxes like this can be bought for 10s. to 15s. each, according to size, and they will last a lifetime.

I have said enough about insects. Now consider some of the other activities you can undertake in your "den". Birds' egg collecting is right "out" today and I, for one, never liked it much anyway. I have already mentioned feathers; another idea would be to collect empty nests after the breeding season is over. Skulls of birds and animals are very interesting to collect and a visit to a gamekeeper's gibbet would probably give you enough raw material to work on for some time. The preparation of a skull may perhaps not be to your taste, but it is not very difficult if you boil it first long enough to loosen the flesh from the bones and then carefully scrape it all off. The best kind of display case for skulls and bones is a shallow box lined with black paper and fitted with a glass lid. An old picture frame could probably be made to fit.

OPENING BAT

SIR LEONARD HUTTON, *Yorkshire's master of style and technique, became England's first professional captain. He has much helpful advice for young cricketers.*

FROM a small boy, opening the innings always held a fascination for me. A new venture begins as you walk out with your partner; a new pitch awaits you, and, of course, a new ball, so deadly in the hands of a good opening bowler. It is much better to walk out with a partner than alone, although the opening batsman's task is the hardest of all. Great comradeship develops between opening partners. You have probably heard of the partnerships of Hobbs and Sutcliffe, or Woodfull and Ponsford. Those great names made their mark with long partnerships, and became the heartache of opening bowlers.

What does the opening batsman think as he sits with his pads on in the dressing-room, waiting for the opposition to take the field? First, he must see that his kit is in first-class order. Remember the new ball is harder than the one that has been used for half an hour. Inadequate protection may result in a serious injury. Try, if possible, to gain information about the two opening bowlers. One may occasionally bowl an off-break as Bob Appleyard, the Yorkshire bowler did, or a slow leg break like Sir "Leary" Constantine, the superb West Indian fast bowler. To know these points is of great help as you walk out to give your team a sound start. It is your job to take the sting out of the opening bowlers, and prepare the way for the lower batsmen who perhaps do not play so correctly as you try to do.

Most opening batsmen are correct players; an opening batsman who plays with a slightly cross bat will make little progress in good-class cricket. The grip with the left hand is very important. This grip should be in a position which makes you use all the muscles in the left arm to the fullest extent. Stand with your feet apart, and place the bat on the ground between your feet with the top of the handle opposite the toes.

Now bend down in the crouch position, placing your hands lightly on the handle so that the two V's formed by the index finger and thumbs are pointing down the splice. This grip will make you use your left arm, bringing every muscle into use as you play each stroke.

Let me take you with me to open the innings for England against Australia. Arriving at the ground, we prepare to have a short knock in the practice nets. This is more or less to loosen up, and accustom ourselves to the light. On our way to the nets we have paused a moment to inspect the middle where the battle is to take place for the following four or five days. Our point in looking at the match wicket is to try to determine what pace it might be. Invariably in England the wicket will be at its quickest, and most dangerous for the swing bowler, in the first two hours of the match.

The opening bowlers may be as formidable as Lindwall and Miller. They will be out for a quick wicket, so we must be prepared to expect hostile bowling. The crowd are keyed up, the bowlers are keen to start the fray, rather like the good boxer all agitated for the first bell; even the umpires will be keyed up to 100 per cent concentration, and we, the opening batsmen, will have a strange feeling of fear, a slight ache, perhaps, in our tummy which has just come from nowhere, the result, perhaps, of the great ovation we have just received. Guard is taken and as we hear the umpire call "Play", the one taking first ball will find the fears, and aches, disappearing as he taps the ground with his favourite piece of willow. Yes, those few little taps on the block hole, with the feel of the bat handle in your hands, instil a quiet, supreme confidence.

Should the match be on a wonderful cricket ground like Melbourne with 75,000 people eagerly awaiting to see the first ball bowled, you will notice a most distracting silence as a famous bowler starts his run with the new ball, bright and red, held lightly between the first and second fingers of his right hand. The ball will move about in the air for the first three or four overs. Our safest plan will be to use the forward defensive shot as much as possible. Our main reason for this will be to reduce the risk of being out l.b.w. to the ball which may pitch outside the off stump, and break back quickly striking our pads which will have been moved across in order to place our head behind the flight of the ball.

If we are pushing forward then we are in the position to attack the over-pitched ball, and in the best possible position to safeguard our wicket against the fury of a Lindwall. It is the good length or overpitched ball with which he will capture our wicket, not the bumper. The bumper will be used but only to pave the way for us to miss the straight good-length or overpitched delivery. Perhaps in his second over, and by this time he will have warmed a little to the job, he will put all he knows behind a well-pitched-up delivery, aiming for the leg stump. The shine on the ball will probably make it move towards the middle stump late in its flight. This ball is a potential wicket taker and a very dangerous one. But we are careful to play the ball in the direction of between the wicket and mid on, or straight back to the bowler.

Keen observation must be the keynote of our early play. Every opportunity must be taken to take the short single which is very disconcerting to the bowler, and will enable us to draw the field closer to the wicket, making it easier to score two's and three's and four's. When we are at the running end of the wicket it is important that we should be backing up. By this I mean we must, immediately the ball has left the bowler's hand, walk at least two yards towards the striker's end. We are then in the best possible position to obtain that quick single, and to turn what might have been only a single into two runs or possibly three.

Before we receive the first ball, however, it is essential that we make a mental note of the field placings. The disposition of the fielders will enable us to obtain good knowledge of what the bowler will be trying to make the ball do. If we are right-handers and see three slips and a gully then we can expect outswingers, but watch carefully for the outswinger which the bowler is bound to try occasionally as a surprise ball.

Good opening bats are scarce. Few have the ability to cope with the swinging ball, or to restrain themselves in the early stages of the innings when self-control is so important to give the team a sound start. It is correct technique which enables you to master the art of batsmanship on all wickets under any conditions. *Give thought to your net work, and avoid being careless.* Practice can be divided into two parts, the first half for defence, the second for attack. In the latter half try to hit the ball as late as possible. Get your power into the shot when the bat has passed the shoulder level on the downward swing. Great players often hit the ball easily. This is because the hitting has been delayed until the last two feet of the downward swing. There is only one part of the bat with which to strike the ball—the middle. If your bat has many cracks down the edges, then you are hitting too early, and possibly lifting the bat too high. Practice is very important. The more effort which you put into your play the more success you will have, and perhaps one day you, too, will have that wonderful feeling of opening for England.

LOOK OUT FOR BEACH JEWELS

by

TREVOR HOLLOWAY

HALF-WAY through your holiday by the sea, having sampled all the usual attractions—boating, bathing, fishing from the end of the pier—you are ready for some new venture. How about trying your luck as an amateur "prospector" in quest of semi-precious stones or "beach jewels"?

I do not suggest that you will make your fortune or even enough cash to pay your ice-cream bills, but there is a sporting chance you may come across a few stones of great beauty which, after being cut and polished, would make a fine brooch or pendant. What is the difference between *precious* and *semi-precious* stones? Only five stones are recognized today as precious—diamonds, rubies, sapphires, emeralds, and precious opals. Needless to say, you won't come across any of them!

Beach jewels are natural stones used in jewellery. They include many that are sufficiently attractive for ornamental purposes—agate, amethyst, aquamarine, topaz, golden beryl, smoky quartz, fluorspar and many more. According to a member of the Gemmological Association, they are gem stones, and a very good quality gem stone *can* be more valuable than a poor quality diamond.

Semi-precious stones are also found at many places inland. Most stones are found along the coast because the sea has pounded away at the rocks and cliffs and done most of the spade-work by exposing the rock-face or breaking it up at the foot of cliffs. The key to success is careful and systematic search. Comb one area thoroughly; it is far better to concentrate on a small area than to flit from place to place like a butterfly. Fresh rock falls at the foot of cliffs and rocky slopes are worth investigating and so are stretches of beach above high-water.

Agate is a stone of great beauty to be found along the shore of Suffolk and at many points around the coast of Scotland. It is one of the most-used of the quartz varieties and colours include milk-white, yellow, red, and brown, and occasionally blue and green. It is essentially a striped stone and therefore fairly easy to identify. Agates having alternate black and white bands are known as onyx; those with brown and white bands are sardonyx. The Suffolk coast is one of Britain's best hunting grounds for beach jewel seekers. Red jasper, which will take a high polish, is most likely to be found at the northern end of the coast round Felixstowe; other parts of the coastline yield amber and jet.

Amber, often washed up on the East Coast, is not a mineral, but an ancient vegetable product produced from certain kinds of long extinct coniferous trees. Colours range from almost white to a dark brown, but the usual colour is honey-brown yellow. Incidently, long-extinct insects and leaves are sometimes to be found embedded in clear amber, so if the material itself may not be of outstanding interest, its contents may well be! Carnelian is found along our North-west coastline and on rocky slopes in North Wales. The stone is often of a yellowish tinge but glows deep orange in strong sunlight.

The rocky coast of Cornwall is second only to the coast of Scotland as a gem-hunter's paradise. Readers on holiday or in reach of these shores should be on the look-out for blue and white aquamarine and also for the lovely malachite with its attractive green colouring derived from contact with copper in the soil. The Cairngorm Mountains, part of the Scottish Grampians, is a region which may justly be called the gem-hunters' paradise. Emeralds of flawless beauty have been picked up in these mountains for centuries. Topaz may also be found, of blue-green or whitish hue, as well as green and golden beryl. On Cairngorm Mountain itself have been found topazes, Cairngorm stones (which are varieties of smoky quartz, reddish-brown or yellowish-brown in colour) much used in Highland jewellery. The extraordinary rock formations of the island of Arran, in the Firth of Clyde, probably harbour a greater variety of gems and pebbles than any other area of similar size in Britain. Amethysts, topazes, a beautiful variety of quartz known as cat's-eye jasper, rose quartz, agate and many other stones are found.

COLLECTING CHEESE LABELS

by

MICHAEL STOREY

CHEESE label collecting, or fromology (the adopted title for the hobby), really started in the early 1920's, when many cheese and dairy concerns made their own collections of labels issued not only on their own cheese products, but also on that of rival manufacturers. Private collectors at this period were few and far between and their numbers dwindled during World War II.

Today fromology is one of the most popular collecting hobbies in Europe. In 1951 a Fromologists' Circle was founded in London. The "Circle" maintains contact with collectors throughout the world and in 1957 introduced a Junior Branch. In order to make the hobby even more popular, it has now set a Control of not more than One Shilling on the price of a scarce label. This is a far cry from the days when certain labels were known to sell for as much as £10 to £50 each! In 1951, the *Société de Tyrosemiophilie* was founded in Paris for French collectors. It is a thriving and widespread organization.

Most countries in the world produce cheese and the most easily collected labels come from the British Isles, Denmark, and Switzerland. Labels from the U.S.S.R., Yugoslavia, Turkey, Japan, Hungary, and Argentina are very scarce and are particularly sought by collectors. Although the majority of fromologists try to obtain a copy of every label, some collectors do specialize. They may collect the labels of a particular country, or they may concentrate on labels of a particular shape or size. Some endeavour to get one label from each different manufacturer or distributor. There is no end to the search for new labels. Every year new ones are issued, and old ones may have the illustration re-drawn or have new wording added—thus producing "varieties". Error printings, too, are now eagerly sought.

Cheese manufacturers are beginning to realize that fromology is helping to sell their cheese. One Swiss concern issues coupons in its packings to promote sales. These coupons can be collected and exchanged for labels unobtainable in this country. Other Swiss firms have even introduced obsolete labels in their boxes of processed cheese. All fromologists will agree that there is plenty of variety among their labels. Sizes range from an oval Czechoslovakian label which measures less than one inch at its widest point to large circular Italian Gorgonzola labels. As for shapes, triangular and circular ones are the most common, but an amazing number of labels of assorted shapes can be collected.

Some very attractive Italian labels have been issued recently. One company in Italy has produced a series depicting photographs of famous International footballers. These are prized very highly by collectors. During the Second World War, chocolate was not easy to procure in Italy, and cheese, having a similar calorie value, was sold in its place. Labels issued on this wartime cheese bore the wording *Surrogato di Cioccolato* ("Substitute for chocolate") and to attract Italian children they were issued in beautifully illustrated sets depicting birds, national costumes, animals and so on. An Austrian firm has now issued a set of six triangular and six circular labels depicting, in many colours, well-known fairy tales by Grimm. One could go on for a long time describing the many wonderful labels that it is now possible to collect.

The labels of Italy are without doubt some of the world's most outstanding examples. They vary from the large circular ones to be found on natural Gorgonzola cheeses to the familiar small labels issued on boxes of processed cheese. Responsible for many of the latter is the firm of Egidio Galbani, for many years well known for the many collectors' items they have produced among their labels, including their famous Crema and Formaggino Sport series, known as *Galbani Footballers*. Certainly no other country goes to such lengths to be original in its labels. Think of a subject and it is almost certain that some Italian company has represented it some way or other on a label. If you are interested in art there are many labels depicting well-known sculptures, paintings, and architecture that should be in your collection. One such label depicts a reproduction of the famous painting, the *Mona Lisa*. Cartoon characters appear on many labels, and those inspired or made famous by Walt Disney are not forgotten: these include *Bambi*, *Cinderella*, and the *Three Little Pigs*.

History is well covered on Italian cheese labels, too. Many famous characters and incidents are depicted. One company, Giovanni Colombo, uses a painting of Christopher Columbus on almost all its labels. Several Italian companies have issued yellow and blue triangular labels.

CAMERA

by

B. J. CHUTE

*Have you ever tried to make an
amateur film? This hilarious story
shows what might happen if you
don't do the job properly!*

"But I tell you, it's stupendous," said Tommy Moore, rising from the depths of a lime juice shake. "It's the opportunity of a lifetime."

"Ha!" Spud Davies stirred the remains of a strawberry sundae and expressed doubt and gloom in an incredulous grunt.

"In the first place," Tommy continued brightly, abandoning the shake with a final gurgle, "all we have to do is get the gang together, and tell 'em we've decided to make a film."

"Sweet word," Spud murmured, sourly.

Tommy ignored him in a loud voice. "Now, what's wrong with *that*?"

"Life," said Spud sardonically, "is too short to tell you. For one thing, we haven't got a ciné-camera. I merely mention it. You may, of course, be planning to use a little black box with a hole in it."

"We'll hire one," Tommy told him, sweepingly. "I know a fellow who said he'd let me hire his camera from him any time I wanted to, and it's a wonderful one—sixteen millimetre film—and I'll be the

42

SHY

director," Tommy went on dreamily, "and Buzz'll be the head cameraman, of course, and somebody'll have to write a script. Me, maybe. Listen, Spud, it's going to be wonderful." He broke off and eyed his friend solicitously. "*Now* what's the trouble?"

"Listen," Spud growled, darkly. "Every time you tell me one of your bright ideas is going to be wonderful, something awful happens."

"But don't you think it *is* going to be wonderful?" said Tommy with an innocent expression.

"I think it's going to be horrible," Spud said.

Tommy's round face registered profound dismay. "But you'll help, won't you?"

"I suppose so," said Spud. "The trouble with me is that I have a heart of solid gold and a head of cotton-wool. And no instinct of self-preservation!"

"You don't need any instinct of self-preservation," Tommy told him comfortingly. "I'll take care of you."

"That," said Spud, "is exactly what I'm afraid of."

*   *   *

The field behind the Moore home bore a striking resemblance to the last days of Pompeii, the San Francisco earthquake, and the Charge of the Light Brigade. It was cluttered up with human forms in various

43

stages of collapse or activity. It was also littered with an assortment of props, costumes and other impedimenta, indicating film production. Under a small elm tree sat Spud, in full cowboy regalia, the sweeping brim of a Stetson hat shading his face, with an expression of the most profound gloom. For six solid hours he had fought passionately against being cast as the hero of *Tex of the Western Range*, and was only won over at last by economic pressure applied by Tommy, who pointed out pathetically that Spud was the only one who fitted the costume they had. Against his better judgment, therefore, Spud finally allowed himself to be arrayed in Western trappings and led before the camera like a lamb to the slaughter. After five days "on location" (as Tommy insisted on calling it), he was sadder than ever.

Near him, on a camp stool, enduring the tender ministrations of the make-up man, sat Alan Blake, cast as the villain of the piece. As the costumier had only been able to produce the one outfit, it had been necessary to clothe the other characters in imagination and ingenuity, to which Alan's ensemble was a striking testimonial. With an old shirt and overalls as a basis, a broad-brimmed hat, belt and motor-cycle gauntlets the costume man had managed to create a very fair effect, but it was the addition of a doormat on each leg, in place of the customary chaps, that really produced the desired glamour. And, as Tommy pointed out, so long as Alan kept his left side toward the camera, the mat with "Welcome" cut into it wouldn't show.

Alan, chaps and all, was gazing trustingly up into the face of Bill Lisle and having a sinister and drooping moustache affixed to his upper lip. This proved to be more of an undertaking than was altogether necessary, as the spirit gum needed at least two minutes of quiet in which to dry, and Alan was incapable of keeping still for that length of time. It fell off for the fourth time. Bill howled and tipped over the make-up box.

"Less noise, please," said Tommy, who was sitting in a chair marked "Director" and being very capable and brisk about everything. He was also wearing his cap back to front, purely for effect, and this irritated Bill so much that he rose to suggest in cold tones that Tommy might come over and fix the moustache himself, if he was so wonderful.

This Tommy declined to do, on the grounds that he was busy, and returned to his occupation of staring into space with a thoughtful and discerning expression.

"Busy doing what?" Bill inquired, rudely.

"I'm visualizing the next scene," said Tommy with hauteur. "Where's the sheriff? We've got to start shooting."

The sheriff, dressed like Alan but with a pair of small Oriental rugs for chaps instead of doormats, came forward, a long grey beard straggling from his hand.

"Better put your beard on, Sam," said Alan, on the sound principle that misery loves company.

Sam obediently raised the foliage, which hooked over his ears, but Tommy interrupted. "Not yet," said Tommy. "Hold on a minute."

"Why not?" said Sam.

"The face," said Tommy, tersely, "has not been prepared."

Sam blinked, struck amidships by the elegance of the director's language. "I *beg* your pardon?"

"The face has not been prepared," Tommy repeated coldly.

"Oh." Light dawned. "You mean, I haven't got my make-up on yet."

"That's what I said."

"No, you didn't. You said—skip it." Sam sat down meekly to wait for Bill to finish with Alan's moustache, and Tommy turned his attention to the cameraman, who was examining the camera and explaining to two terriers and a bulldog the difference between Chromatic and Spherical Aberration.

Tommy interrupted this domestic scene to announce that they would be ready to shoot in a minute, and was he ready? Buzz Adams said he was always ready, and then proceeded to rush around focusing the camera, cleaning the lens and falling over the bulldog. Tommy glanced at his watch, and looked through the script which was spread out on his knees. "We'll take Sequence Six—the big hold-up scene between Jasper Dean and the sheriff, where Tex rides in and saves the gold."

"You can't save gold nowadays," Spud remarked, waking up. "It's against the law."

"*Will* you shut up?" said Tommy, unjustly, as this was Spud's first remark of the afternoon. "We'll roll 'em in five minutes."

"Roll them?" Buzz murmured vaguely.

"The cameras."

Buzz looked at his lone camera, gazed around as if expecting to find another, and then said "Oh" in a respectful voice and pushed a terrier out of his way.

The result of Tommy's stern order was that, at the end of half an hour, the actors were properly made up, the debris had been cleared away from the scene of action, and a large wooden packing case, on which was printed "TOMATO SOUP—HANDLE WITH CARE" in large letters, had been hauled into range of the camera, in front of a row of bushes.

Tommy got to his feet and yelled for attention. "Now, look," he said earnestly, having got it. "This is about the biggest scene in the whole film, and it's got to be good." He sat down again, elbows on knees, and fixed the cast with a glittering eye. "We've rehearsed it, but I'll go over it again for you. Here's the picture. Fade-in. The sheriff crouching in the bushes, rifle in hand, guarding the precious box of gold——"

"Box of soup," Alan interjected. "Listen Tommy, don't you think we ought to get a different kind of packing-case? That tomato soup sign looks queer to me."

"I don't see why," said Tommy. "If we're trying to hide some gold, why wouldn't it be intelligent to put it in a packing-case that had been used for soup and make everyone think it was——"

"Bouillon, instead of bullion," Spud cracked, suddenly becoming animated. "Boy, am I clever?"

Tommy rewarded this effort with a dirty look. "Anyway," he said, "nobody'd think of suspecting a packing-case marked soup."

"Especially not when there's a sheriff crouched over it with a gun in his hands," Alan agreed, politely. "Never mind. Go on."

"So," Tommy continued, undisturbed, "he's crouching there, and all of a sudden he hears a noise in the bushes. He turns his head, listening intently. Close-up of Jasper, lurking behind a tree, a revolver in his hand. Then a medium-shot of the sheriff, still listening——"

"One-track mind he's got," said Alan. "Get on with it, Tommy. I have some important lurking to do."

"Oh, well, you know the business in there anyway," Tommy said with a sigh. "You come out and hold the sheriff up and, just as you're about to shoot him, we fade to a long shot of Tex, riding towards you at a gallop. I say!" He twisted around in his chair to address Dick Ellison, the prop man. "You have got the horse, haven't you?"

There was a short silence. "Well, yes," said Dick, doubtfully. "I have. He's in the barn."

"Good. We'll get a long shot of Tex riding across the meadow—that'll be okay, won't it, Buzz?" Receiving an approving nod, he went on. "Then we come in again on the sheriff and Jasper, and just as Jasper raises his gun, Tex swings his lariat and lassos the villain."

46

"I have never used a lariat in my life," Spud interrupted, realistically. "I'll probably lasso a tree—or the sheriff."

"You don't understand modern miracles," Tommy told him patiently. "We shoot you——"

"What have *I* done?"

"Photograph you," said Tommy, grimly, "spinning the rope. And then we sh— photograph the rope whirling through the air, and then we show it settled over Jasper's arms. The audience does all the in-between part for us, in their own imaginations."

"Marvellous, Holmes, marvellous. The camera cannot lie."

"Okay, let's get going. Now, remember, this is our big scene, and it's got to be good. Give it everything you've got."

"*I've* got a feeling," Spud announced in an aside to Alan.

"What kind of a feeling?" Alan asked, concernedly.

"What the writers call Impending Doom," said Spud, dejectedly. "I foresee trouble in this sequence. I feel it in my bones."

"Are we ready?" Tommy shouted, so loudly that he startled even himself. "Ready, Buzz?"

"Yes."

"Okay, sheriff. Action!"

* * *

Two close-ups went off successfully, and Tommy called "Cut" in a pleased voice. "Okay now, Buzz. Medium-shot, getting them both in. This is big stuff. Try to get it right first time, so we don't have to make a re-take. It saves film."

Sam, in charge of the accounts when not impersonating the sheriff, made an approving noise, and Tommy turned to Buzz, who had been measuring distances, squinting at the sun, and focusing his lens with a most professional air. "Ready, Buzz?"

Buzz beamed. "Let 'em roll."

"Action! Camera!" Tommy interrupted himself with an upraised hand. "Wait a second. We'll have music with this scene, just to get the mood right."

Dick, who was the orchestra, as well as property man, pawed through a pile of odds and ends and produced a battered-looking harmonica. "What must I play?"

"Something sinister and dashing," Tommy suggested, hopefully.

"Would 'Happy Days Are Here Again' be all right?" said Dick.

"Jumping crocodiles, no! What's sinister about that?" Tommy demanded. "Don't you know *anything* else?"

"How about 'Marching Through Georgia' in waltz time?"

This brilliant effort inspired a chorus of suggestions.

"How about shutting up?" said Tommy. "We'll have 'Happy Days' if we must, only try to make it sound threatening, will you? Okay—action! Camera! Everyone set? Go!"

With Jasper lurking and the sheriff listening, they began all over again. The sheriff, who, because of the requirements of the script, was not too bright at the best, obligingly listened in the wrong direction, and Alan, alias Jasper Dean, parted the bushes and stole forth with a menacing expression, his revolver pointing at the officer's back.

"Stick 'em up, yuh dog!" said Tommy, marking the place for Title on his script and getting the astonished attention of the actors. "No!" he wailed. "Don't stop acting, you dopes. I was just saying the sub-title. Cut!"

Buzz stopped grinding, and the agitated director breathed heavily. "Now we'll have to take that over again," he mourned. "Listen, you, don't ever stop acting unless you hear me say 'Cut'."

He vanished once more behind his tree, Dick struck up Happy Days again, and the sheriff cocked an ear. This time they got safely past the sub-title; the sheriff whirled around to find himself gazing dramatically into the muzzle of a revolver, made a gesture to raise his rifle, received a stern glare, and slowly, slowly, in response to a silent but unyielding command, let the weapon drop from his hand.

"Sneer at him, Jasper," the director advised, making cooing noises of contented appreciation.

Jasper sneered obediently, but unfortunately with such enthusiasm that his moustache, a tender flower at best, promptly fell at his feet.

"Cut!" said Tommy, almost with a sob. "We'll have to have a re-take."

Bill Lisle, in a paroxysm of temper and regret, used up nearly all the spirit gum on the defaulting ornament, and Jasper and the sheriff grimly started the scene again, after allowing time for the sheriff to estimate how much film had been wasted. Finally, they got through the scene successfully, sneer and all, and Tommy shouted a grateful "Cut!" and leaned back in his chair exhausted.

"All right, now," he said, recovering slightly. "Long shot of Tex, galloping across the field. Dick, go and get the horse."

Dick eyed the director rather strangely, swallowed hard and dis-

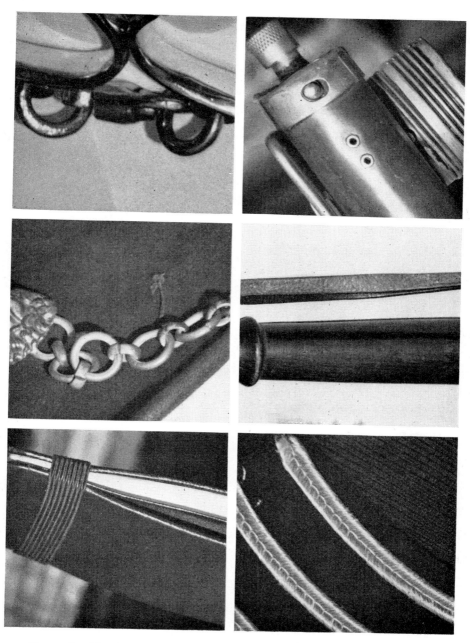

PLATE 2. Here's a PHOTO QUIZ set by DAVID PETERS. The six photos are all connected with one career. Identify the career and the items in a time limit of five minutes. Solution on page 191.

PLATE 3. (Above) Model of the Curtiss-Wright propeller-driven train which will carry 276 passengers in 3 coaches. (Below) The s.s. *Rotterdam* (38,645 tons) has no funnels; twin exhausters replace them.

appeared in the direction of the barn. In a few minutes, he returned with what he *said* was a horse. No one believed him. Tommy gave it one look and reeled over backwards, chair and all. Spud had a fit of hysterics on the spot, and the two terriers and the bulldog rushed around in circles, barking madly. The horse peered around the scene with a benign and slightly forlorn expression, then rubbed its nose gently on Dick's shirt and nudged his shoulder.

"Do you call *that* a horse?" Tommy demanded, as soon as he could get his voice back.

"What's wrong with it?" said Dick indignantly. "If you ask me, it's a pretty good horse."

"A pretty good horse!" Tommy howled. "A pretty good camel, maybe, or giraffe! But a horse!" He shook his head violently. "You can't stand there and tell me that's a horse. I know better."

"What's wrong with it?" Dick repeated, grimly.

Tommy, calmer now, regarded the animal appraisingly. "Well," he said finally, in a judicial manner, "it's knock-kneed and hunch-backed. It can hardly walk, much less gallop. It's as wide as a barn door, and has just about as much spirit. And it looks like an accident. Otherwise it's the most beautiful hippopotamus I've ever seen."

Dick, who was forced to admit a certain amount of truth in these remarks, stroked the subject's nose and said defensively that he'd been able to get this particular horse dirt cheap. Sam, as the anxious custodian of the cash, immediately saw hitherto unobserved beauties in the animal, and began an eloquent defence.

"Well," Tommy conceded finally, gazing at the horse which was chewing quietly at a lilac tree, "I'll tell you what we'll do. If we can get this horse to gallop—which I don't think we can—we'll use it." He turned to Buzz. "You get a shot of them as they sweep across," he said, "and then a head-on shot as they come up to where the sheriff and Jasper are. It's going to knock the audience right out of their seats."

"Sweep, eh?" said Spud.

"Head-on, eh?" said Buzz.

"That's right." Tommy was very calm about everything. "All right, now. All set?"

Spud cleared his throat doubtfully. "Look," he said, "I don't think for a second that anything'll make that horse move any faster than a snail, but if it does, how do I stay on?"

Tommy gazed upon his friend with genuine interest. "Haven't you ridden before?"

Spud shook his head.

"Oh, well," said Tommy, "there's nothing to it. You'll find you just stick on naturally. It has something to do with gravity or centrifugal force or something. Nothing to it at all."

"Have you ever ridden?" Spud asked, with suspicious gentleness.

"Well, not exactly." Tommy admitted. "But I know it's very simple. Besides," he added with a touch of inspiration, "look how mild the old fellow is. You don't think *he's* going to tip you off, do you, Spud? A gentle old thing like that?"

"Yes," said Spud, grimly. "I do."

Then, with an heroic expression and a fond farewell all round, he proceeded to mount—a preliminary which required an astonishing amount of assistance and which bored the horse profoundly. Once aboard, he felt happier, and let out a loud "Yippee", at the same time kicking the horse with his heel.

The motion made him lose his stirrup, and the horse unexpectedly started forward at an ungainly trot. Gently but firmly, Spud slid off its tail. After this, he refused to re-mount, and it was Sam's turn to argue, since it was quite clear to Sam that, mounted or unmounted, they were paying cash for the privilege of the horse's companionship.

"Hold on to the saddle when it starts to run," Dick advised in a kindly manner. "It won't show—much—in the picture, and you'll feel a lot safer."

Spud made a small sad noise, and allowed himself to be hoisted upwards once more. With magnificent courage, he clucked his tongue and gave his mount a gentle slap with the reins.

Nothing happened. He tried again, with the same results. Tommy meditated a moment, then went around behind to administer a little encouragement. It was, however, quite unnecessary. Just at that moment, the smaller terrier took matters into its own jaws and, apparently irritated by this large and stationary animal, ran in suddenly and gave it a nip on the off foreleg. Spud felt a convulsive earthquake taking place underneath him, as his steed heaved upwards, and he just had time to get a good grip on the saddle before the scenery began to whizz past.

Tommy glanced hastily at Buzz, to be sure the cameraman was getting this splendid piece of action, and then gave his admiring attention to the scene. "Do you know," he said, wonderingly, "I never thought he had it in him."

This happy contemplation was changed to sudden horror, as the gallant cowboy and his four-footed friend crashed through the Moore's fence, got involved with the clothes line and, taking most of Monday's wash with them, disappeared from sight. There was a moment's tense silence, while cast and crew stared in a wild surprise; then pandemonium broke out once more as Spud and the horse again swung into view, Spud bouncing up and down like an impassioned pea and the horse laying itself out and covering more space at a time than seemed altogether cautious or necessary.

Buzz, still grinding grimly, caught them in flight, just as Spud went by shouting "Make him stop!" and just before they went through a cold frame.

"They're coming this way again!" Dick shouted, dodging behind a tree. "That animal thinks he's on a merry-go-round or something. Look out! Buzz!"

As horse and rider swept by, Dick and Alan picked Buzz up and tried kindly to brush him down.

"Keep on grinding!" Tommy yelled. "Boy, what a shot! Get it, Buzz! Here they come! Thunder and lightning, they're going through the fence again!"

Alan made a sound like a foghorn in pain, and slapped a hand to his brow. "They're going to *jump* it!" he wailed in honest anguish.

Incredibly, he was right. The horse, having tried going through the fence once and not liking the experience, was now planning to go *over* it. Spud gave one sorrowful wail and closed his eyes.

The horse rose. The rider fell. They picked Spud tenderly out of the lilac tree, and the horse, relieved of its burden, peered over the fence in a kindly manner. Spud occupied five minutes counting his bruises and giving Tommy dirty looks. When he could trust himself to speak, he said, almost with a note of content, "Well, that lets *me* out. You'll have to get somebody who can ride. Come and see me sometime when I'm convalescent." He got stiffly to his feet, and added "Ouch" in a bitter voice.

Tommy gazed at him, all wide-eyed innocence. "But you were wonderful," said Tommy. "We'll use all these shots, and go on from there. I'll just rewrite the scene."

"You'll *what*?"

"Rewrite the scene." He waved his arms excitedly. "Look, we'll change it like this. Instead of your riding up and getting Jasper in this part. Jasper sees you coming and—just as you're about to leap the fence—he raises his gun. A shot rings out. You fall."

51

He paused, beaming proudly. "That explains your falling off, you see."

"Oh. *That* explains my falling off, does it?" said Spud, through his teeth.

"Sure. It'll be a riot—the best scene we've got." Tommy's face grew thoughtful. "Then, after that, we'll have another big scene, with you on the horse, where you really do rescue the gold. That's after you recover from your wound."

"After I——! Listen." Spud squeaked in indignation. "If you think you're going to bamboozle me into getting astride that—that fire-eating camel again, you——"

"It was wonderful," said Tommy, gently. "Simply wonderful. We'll take the next scene now."

THE KNIGHT'S GAME

Here is a "simple" puzzle, but quite a teaser. Most people find it hard to stop once they tackle it. On a sheet of paper draw a block of 64 squares—that is 8 by 8—about the size of a crossword puzzle. Now, with a pencil, just fill in the numbers 1 to 64. You may begin anywhere but using only this move: you must always put your next number two squares forwards and one square sideways *or* one square forwards and two squares sideways. This is the Knight's move in chess but it doesn't matter if you can't play chess. Your start may look something like this:

			2	5			
	1				4		
			3	6			

Not more than one figure may appear in any one square. Now try it . . . and it can be done! (*One solution appears on page 191*)

Boy's Own WORKSHOP

Designed by
P. W. BLANDFORD

Most of us like to make things. While the simplest articles can be made with very little equipment—perhaps just a knife and file, used on a table or desk—we need a workshop to tackle anything ambitious. Even if at first a place of your own is out of the question some sort of portable equipment which can be stowed away is a first step. The Boy's Own Workshop has been designed to guide you. The tools you will need have been drawn and described in detail. With this foundation you can go on for many happy hours doing it yourself. First of all you will need a bench.

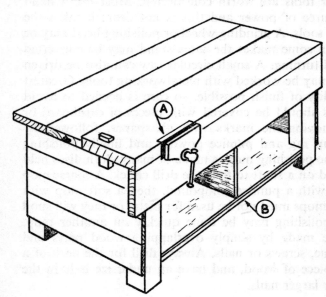

A bench will be much firmer than any table. Stiffen the front edge by an apron piece and use a flush-fitting woodworking vice (*fig.* A). Have the main plank of the top about $1\frac{1}{2}$ in. thick and legs about 2 in. square or larger. Framing up the bottom by fitting shelves or cupboards makes it more rigid (*fig.* B) The smallest worth-while vices have 6 in. jaws for woodwork, 2 in. jaws for metal.

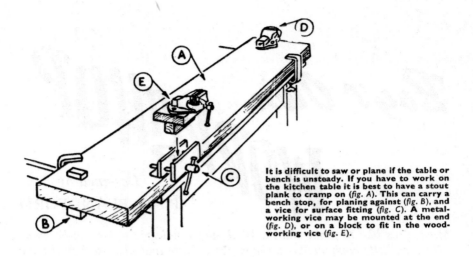

It is difficult to saw or plane if the table or bench is unsteady. If you have to work on the kitchen table it is best to have a stout plank to cramp on (fig. A). This can carry a bench stop, for planing against (fig. B), and a vice for surface fitting (fig. C). A metal-working vice may be mounted at the end (fig. D), or on a block to fit in the wood-working vice (fig. E).

As the materials you are most likely to deal with are wood, metal and plastics, your main concern is a kit of woodworking tools, with a few basic metalworking ones. Tin cans may be cut up and made into many things. The material, thin sheet iron coated on both sides with tin, solders easily. Common solder, bought in sticks, is a mixture of lead and tin. Small power tools are worth considering. Most use a hand electric drill as a source of power and this is not dear; it takes the place of several hand tools. A grinding wheel or polishing head may be fitted in the chuck. In some makes the same stand may be converted into a lathe for wood turning. A small circular saw can also be driven by the drill. Plastics may be worked with metalworking tools. Greatest attraction is the quality of finish possible, so care is needed to avoid scratching. Vice jaws should be covered with pieces of cardboard or fibre. Finish by removing file marks with glasspaper, followed by scouring with a damp rag and pumice powder and finally polishing with metal polish. The polishing mop is made of many cloth discs held together and mounted on a shaft to fit in the drill chuck. A coarse mop should be used first with a pumice compound, then a soft mop with finishing polish. The mops must not be used for metal or they will spoil the plastics. Metal polishing may be done quickly on another mop. Many things can be made by simply overlapping wood parts and joining them with glue, screws or nails. Always drill for the neck of a screw in the upper piece of wood, and have an undersize hole in the lower piece. Drill for larger nails.

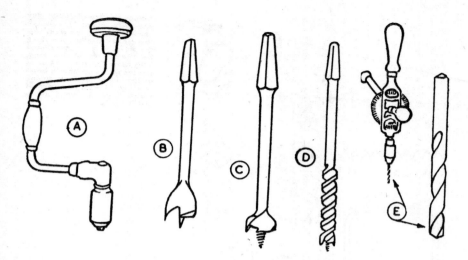

The ordinary brace (fig. A) will take bits to drill holes from ¼ in. upwards. Ordinary centre bits are cheapest (fig. B), but those with screw centres lessen the labour (fig. C) and twist bits are better for deep holes (fig. D). For smaller holes, Morse-pattern twist bits in a wheel brace are better (fig. E).

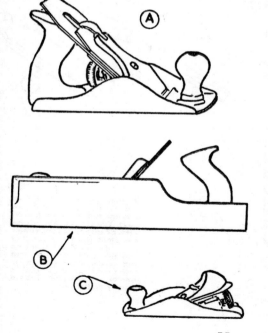

The keen woodworker has a large collection of planes. Small wooden ones are cheap, but very difficult for a beginner to set, and it is better to pay rather more and get a steel plane. Size 4 will do for the first plane (fig. A). This has adjustments for the projection and tilt of the blade. A smoothing plane can be used for many other jobs. Next a wooden jack plane (fig. B) useful for the first smoothing of a sawn or rough surface. For ship modelling or other fine work, a small steel block plane (fig. C) is useful, and cheap.

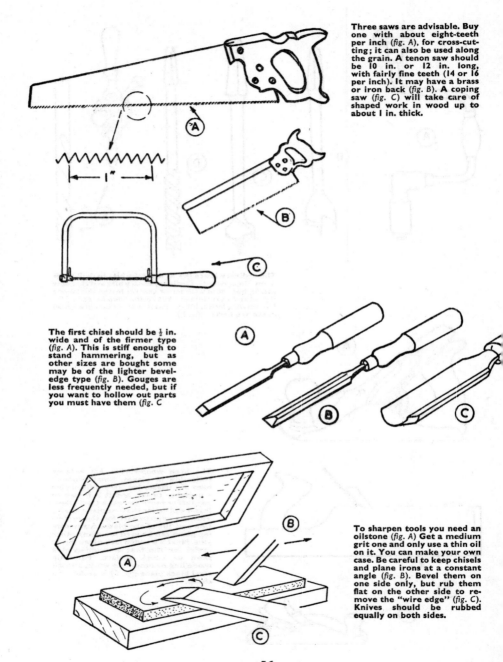

Three saws are advisable. Buy one with about eight-teeth per inch (*fig. A*), for cross-cutting; it can also be used along the grain. A tenon saw should be 10 in. or 12 in. long, with fairly fine teeth (14 or 16 per inch). It may have a brass or iron back (*fig. B*). A coping saw (*fig. C*) will take care of shaped work in wood up to about 1 in. thick.

The first chisel should be ½ in. wide and of the firmer type (*fig. A*). This is stiff enough to stand hammering, but as other sizes are bought some may be of the lighter bevel-edge type (*fig. B*). Gouges are less frequently needed, but if you want to hollow out parts you must have them (*fig. C*

To sharpen tools you need an oilstone (*fig. A*) Get a medium grit one and only use a thin oil on it. You can make your own case. Be careful to keep chisels and plane irons at a constant angle (*fig. B*). Bevel them on one side only, but rub them flat on the other side to remove the "wire edge" (*fig. C*). Knives should be rubbed equally on both sides.

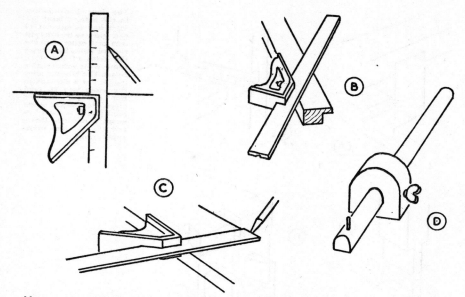

Most marking out will be done with a pencil, but for accurate work a knife is better. A steel rule is better than a wooden one. A combination square can take the place of many tools. It will mark right-angles (fig. A) or mitres (fig. B). Its blade is a rule and a spirit level may be included in the stock. With a pencil against the end it can be used as a marking gauge (fig. C), but a proper marking gauge is cheap and a big help in drawing lines parallel to an edge (fig. D).

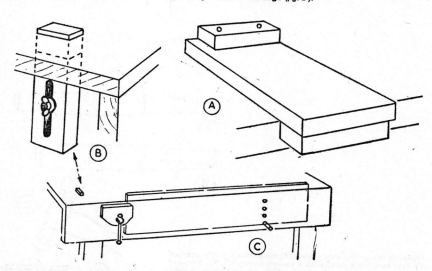

One of the first jobs with the new tools should be the making of a pair of bench hooks (fig. A). These are needed when sawing on the bench and for holding wood for many operations. A stop for planing against is another essential (fig. B). Holes in the apron piece allow pegs to be fitted to support long boards (fig. C).

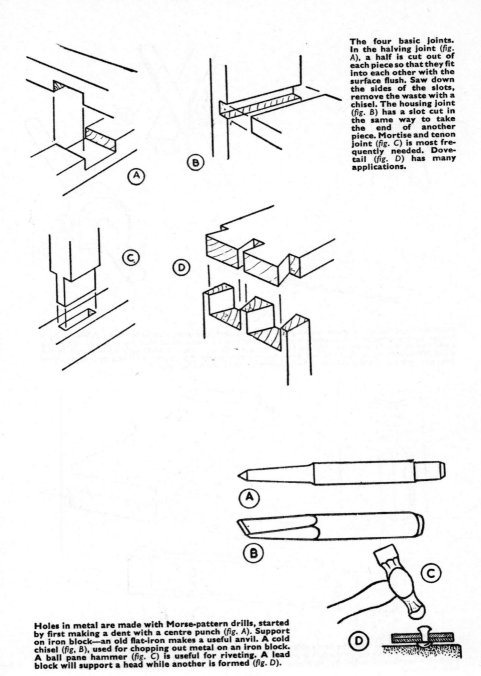

The four basic joints. In the halving joint (fig. A), a half is cut out of each piece so that they fit into each other with the surface flush. Saw down the sides of the slots, remove the waste with a chisel. The housing joint (fig. B) has a slot cut in the same way to take the end of another piece. Mortise and tenon joint (fig. C) is most frequently needed. Dovetail (fig. D) has many applications.

Holes in metal are made with Morse-pattern drills, started by first making a dent with a centre punch (fig. A). Support on iron block—an old flat-iron makes a useful anvil. A cold chisel (fig, B), used for chopping out metal on an iron block. A ball pane hammer (fig. C) is useful for riveting. A lead block will support a head while another is formed (fig. D).

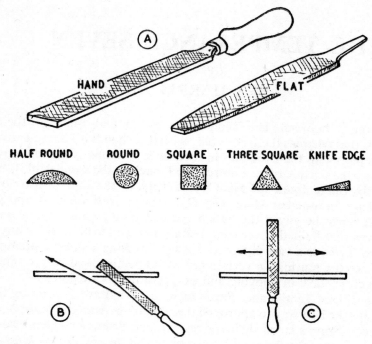

HAND

FLAT

HALF ROUND   ROUND   SQUARE   THREE SQUARE KNIFE EDGE

Basic metalworking tool is the file. There are many types (fig. A) in many lengths and cuts. Start with a second-cut 10 in. hand file. A few others in the same size, but of different sections are useful, and you will soon find a need for some smaller ones, and one or two big ones for rough work. Hold a file at opposite ends and stand to one side. Use a swinging stroke, but keep the file level (fig. B). To smooth an edge draw file with the file sideways (fig. C).

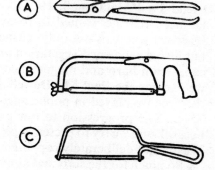

Mild steel ("iron") is cheap and suitable for many purposes. Brass is a more pleasant metal to file and drill. Copper is best for beaten work. Pure aluminium alloys are strong and light. Lead is only useful where weight is needed. It is soft and weak. A pair of tinsnips are needed for cutting sheet metal (fig. A). For thicker metal you need a hacksaw (fig. B). A Junior hacksaw (fig. C) is useful for fine work.

THE TEMPERANCE SEVEN

by

REX HARRIS

THE difference between **The Temperance Seven** and most of their imitators is that whereas these boys play with their hands on their hearts, the others play with their tongues in their cheeks. Nobody could enjoy a whole-hearted parody of jazz more than I, such as the wonderful skits produced by **Spike Jones and His City Slickers,** or the superb satire of **Stan Freburg** in numbers like *The Old Payola Roll Blues* (Capitol CL 15122), when he guyed the "Teen-age idol man", whose sole claim to fame was that he had never sung before, but was willing to try anything once. There is a vast difference between making a sincere attempt to reproduce the music of a certain era with affection and regard, and the much easier task of copying and exaggerating its weakness.

Who *are* these Temperance Seven men, and what are they trying to do? Perhaps the best way to approach these fugitives from the Ballspond Road Cocoa Rooms is via their spokesman and drummer **Brian Innes,** although I am sure that he would much prefer his designation as *Master of the Grand Percussion Kit*. He also claims (but here enters a certain amount of dubiety) the title of *Professor Emeritus and formerly occupier of the Chair of Percussive Studies, Witwatersrand University*.

Persuaded to remain serious for a few minutes, an achievement rare in dealing with any member of this volatile and happy band, he recalled: "It was Christmas 1955, and I was at home doing nothing in particular when there was a tap at the window. I looked out, and there was my friend **Paul MacDowell.** He talked me into allowing him in and announced that he wanted to form a band. He took me to meet **Philip Harrison** who was not only master of the alto and baritone saxophone, but also a renowned vegetarian and inventor of the clockwork hansom cab, steam harp and magnetic corkscrew. With some other enthusiasts we became the **Paul MacDowell Jazzmen** for one appearance only. By the time we played in public again, we were known as the Temperance Seven. The progression to our present form of music has been purely natural, and we try to present a picture of a dance orchestra of the 1920's. We are not deliberately copying—rather, we are interpreting."

So much for the start and aims of this alarming group. Did you know

60

that the leader, trumpeter and euphoniumist **Captain Cephas Howard,** had a distinguished military career during which he was awarded the Charing Cross (with bar), the Last Order (with bar), and the Alhambra Star (nothing barred)? Most unfortunately he was unhappily cashiered for gross misappropriation of five *chassepot* rifles and a billiard table. Now at large, he compensates for his defalcations by his trumpet voluntaries, which must be heard to be believed. Joking apart, his nimble fingering is dexterous, and his *embouchure* is in no way muffled by his magnificent beard.

Tricycle Race Record Holder

Let us now move on to **Alan Swainston Cooper,** who claims distinction as the only pedalling clarinettist in existence. He plays clarinet, pedal clarinet, soprano saxophone and phonofiddle, and is the holder of the tricycle record run from London to Brighton in 1903. (Considering that this took place some forty years before he was born, this is indeed a record!) I now introduce **Sheik Haroun Wadi el John R. T. Davies,** an old friend of mine despite the fact that he claims to be Astronomer Royal to the late Kemal Attaturk and collaborator with Thomas Alvar Edison. When interviewed he said that he had three times swum the Channel to the discomfiture of the Dover Customs and Excise Officers. (This I take leave to question: only *twice* has he swum

If ever you see this poster displayed in your town you can be sure there is an evening of fun in store

61

the Channel, and each time he was arrested and fined for having smoked salmon in his enormous calabash. The case was hushed-up because of his invention of the Davies Submarine Escape Appliance —technically secret, but which involved the use of think-balloons.)

Canon Colin Bowles, another distinguished member and ex-member, was an unfrocked member of the British Matchbox Label and Booklet Society. He did, however, endeavour to atone by his foundership of the British and Empire Free-style Balloon Society. His two-handed piano style added much to the popularity of this band, introducing a fantastically new approach to jazz. This use of both hands was subsequently taken up by more seriously minded musicians, creating great possibilities in the interpretation of Bach, Beethoven, Brahms, etc.

It is not generally known that the personal manservant to the Keeper of the Eddystone Lighthouse was **Dr. John Gieves-Watson**—banjoist and holder of the Bardic Crown Llanfairfach Eisteddfod 1902, nor that **Frank Paverty** (pronounced "ffry") is the band's distinguished sousaphonist (pronounced "sous*aff*onist" or "sous*aphon*ist" as you prefer). He claims that he is an undischarged millionaire famed for his feats on the high-wire, and for his troop of performing sealions which he trained in three weeks while taking part in a one-wheeled bicycle race.

Now we pass on (amid vociferous applause) to the one and only **Whispering Paul MacDowell,** master of the megaphone vocals, Ambassador Extraordinary to the Outer Hebrides, distinguished sword-swallower and dancer, but perhaps best known as an embezzler of international standing. Never, perhaps, in the whole history of recorded music has there been such a phenomenon of absolute zero whose utterances have succeeded in producing sounds which will eventually return to the oblivion which is their natural environment. This is in no way a denigration of his achievements, which are, to do him credit, the most accurate reproduction of the banalities of the Twenties.

He is so good that he must be heard to be believed, and those of us who actually remember the days of the General Strike, Put and Take, and *My Chili Bom-Bom* hear in his reconstructions the echoes of our youth. You, too, who are living it up at the moment will feel the same about today's jazz in the year 2000, and the best of luck to you. The Band claims that it "arrived" socially at the epic occasion of the Bournemouth Centenary Celebrations of 1910, when they were awarded the *Prix D'Honneur* for their original rendering of the new dance craze *The Kaiser Rag*. However, having been honoured by a rendering of this historic piece, I regret to say that it is a plagiarism or variation (or, to put it quite bluntly) a *copy* of *Tiger Rag*, which is well known to all students of Jazz as having been written by either Nick La Rocca or Jelly Roll Morton or W. C. Handy or Jack Carey or A. N. Other or a gentleman with the curious name of *Trad.*

The Early Daze of Jazz

All fooling apart, the Temperance Seven has done more to bring back the fun into jazz than any other band. At times we all tend to get rather serious about our jazz music, and we put it into special watertight compartments, forgetting that its whole basis is a carefree attitude. They have given us a fresh approach, and we must thank them for it. Having listened to jazz for some forty years I feel that I am qualified to recommend two of their records which have been released up to the time of writing. They are *You're Driving Me Crazy/Charlie My Boy* (Parlophone 45R 4757) and *Pasadena/Sugar* (Parlophone 45R 4781). These are two discs which will prove their honest approach to the real jazz which has inspired them. An LP entitled *The Temperance Seven 1961* (Parlophone PNC 1152) illustrates their whole-hearted zest in jazz. But if you attend one of their immensely popular concerts you will probably be given a pencil with the programme. They rarely make up their mind what to play until the time comes!

SPORTS QUIZ

UNUSUAL and often interesting names are given to many sports grounds in Britain. We have listed some of them covering football only—Association football (or soccer) and both kinds of Rugby football, the amateur Rugby Union game and the professional Rugby League. Below is a list of 16 football grounds. Name the clubs which play on them and check your list afterwards with the correct solution.

1. The Hawthorns. **2.** The Willows. **3.** The Vetch Field. **4.** The Brewery Field. **5.** The Rectory Field. **6.** Vicarage Road. **7.** Watersheddings. **8.** Deepdale. **9.** Franklin's Gardens. **10.** Eton Avenue. **11.** The Den. **12.** The Firs. **13.** The Reddings. **14.** Grange Road. **15.** Dean Court. **16.** Raeburn Place.

(*Solution on page 191*)

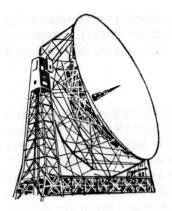

SIGNALS
FROM
OUTER SPACE

by

PATRICK MOORE

CAN we receive messages from outer space? Is it possible that other intelligent races, living millions of millions of miles away, are trying to call up Earth by means of radio? It sounds a fantastic theory, but a team of radio astronomers working in America may be able to tell us whether it is absurd or not. At the National Radio Observatory at Green Bank, West Virginia, Dr. Frank Drake and his colleagues are making a thorough search for such messages from space. They are using first-class modern equipment, and their programme has the full support of the United States Government.

Before explaining just what Dr. Drake and his colleagues hope to do, let us say something about the chances of life in the Universe. Our Earth is a very junior member of the Sun's family; of the other eight planets in the Solar System only Mars and Venus appear able to support life in any form. Mars may have nothing more impressive than lowly plant-stuff, while life on Venus is likely to be confined to primitive sea-creatures, if, indeed, Venus contains any life at all. Yet other suns may well have planet-families of their own, and there is good evidence that such planets exist.

Unfortunately, direct proof is hard to obtain. A planet has no light of its own; it is also small compared with a normal star, and a planet the size of Jupiter moving round a relatively "close" star such as Proxima Centauri (distance about 24 million million miles) would be too faint to be seen even with the world's largest telescope. A planet no larger than our Earth would be impossible to detect.

This means that we have to fall back upon indirect evidence. The Sun is a normal star, and our stellar system or Galaxy contains vast numbers of suns very similar to it. Moreover, there are thousands of millions of other galaxies, so far away that their light—moving at 186,000 miles per second—takes millions of years to reach us. In all this host of stars, it is surely unreasonable to think that the Sun alone is accompanied by an inhabited planet.

We do not know just how life on Earth began; many theories have been put forward, but none is wholly satisfactory. However, there is every reason to believe that life will appear anywhere where conditions are suitable for it. If we find a planet similar to the Earth, experiencing the same temperature range, provided with water, and surrounded by a breathable atmosphere, we may expect it to support living creatures.

Direct contacts with these "other men" are out of the question, so far as we are concerned, because of the distance-scale. Beyond the Solar System there is a tremendous gap before we come to the nearest star, and a journey there, in any kind of space-ship which we can picture, would take many centuries. The only possible means of communication is by radio. Radio waves travel at the same speed as light, and take just over four years to reach us from the nearest star. Sirius, one of the closest of the really brilliant stars, is 8½ "light-years" away; Rigel in Orion seems to be well over 500 light-years distant, and so on.

There is no evidence that the Solar System has ever been contacted by intelligent beings from outer space. Everyone has heard of the flying saucer stories, but when these stories are closely examined they are found to prove nothing at all; and even if flying saucers exist in any form, they are certainly not visiting space-ships. Dr. Drake and his team are not wasting their time on such matters. They are keeping a watch by means of the Green Bank 84-foot radio telescope, which is a very different programme. Moreover, they are concentrating on one definite wavelength, which seems to be much the most promising.

We know that radiations of all kinds reach us from space. There is visible light; there are short-wave radiations, such as X-rays; and there are radiations of longer wave-length, known generally as radio waves. These radio waves are not artificial, and in some ways the name is a misleading one. They are collected by special instruments known as radio telescopes, in much the same way as an ordinary telescope collects light. No visible image is produced, but the results are just as valuable from a scientific point of view. It has been said that a radio telescope is really in the nature of a large aerial. The biggest instrument of the "dish" type has been set up at Jodrell Bank, near Manchester, and is 250 feet across. Not all radio telescopes are of this sort, but all have their own particular advantages and disadvantages.

The space between the stars is not empty. It contains clouds of rarefied, very cold hydrogen gas, and this hydrogen is sending out radiations on a wave-length of 21·1 centimetres. The story of how the radiations were discovered is interesting. During the last war, the Dutch astronomer van de Hulst predicted them theoretically, but at that time Holland was still occupied by the Germans, and no scientific work was possible. It was only in 1951 that two Americans, Ewen and Purcell, managed to detect the 21·1-centimetre radiation, just as van de Hulst had predicted.

Now let us go back to the Green Bank experiment. It is clear that the wave-length of 21·1 centimetres is important throughout the universe; it is characteristic of the hydrogen clouds. If there are any other intelligent races, and if these races have radio equipment as good as ours, they too will be studying the 21·1-centimetre radiation. So if they want to send messages into space, this will be the wave-length which they will choose. For this reason, Dr. Drake and his team are concentrating on this "hydrogen wave-length". If they detect any signals which form a regular pattern, and which cannot be explained by natural phenomena, they will have established that we are not alone in the universe.

It may be possible to narrow down the search still more. Of the relatively nearby stars, two—known to astronomers as Epsilon Eridani and Tau Ceti—are not unlike the Sun, though both are slightly cooler and considerably less luminous. It seems, then, that these two stars are suitable as centres of planetary systems. Whether either has a planet-family, we cannot tell; but it seems a reasonable bet, and so the Green Bank workers have attempted to send out "pulses" on the 21·1-centi-metre wave-length, arranging them so that they could be received by astronomers in the Epsilon Eridani or Tau Ceti systems.

Even supposing that a reply could be received, there will be a long time-lag. Both stars are about eleven light-years away. Therefore, a radio signal will take eleven years to reach them, and the reply would take a further eleven years. This means that even at best, it would be 1983 before a reply could be received to a message transmitted now.

Epsilon Eridani and Tau Ceti are both visible to the unaided eye, and you will be able to find them without difficulty, though neither is at all prominent. Both are yellowish in hue, though a telescope will be needed to show the colours. We must not become over-optimistic, and we have to admit that the chances of success are very slight. There is no proof that Epsilon Eridani and Tau Ceti are accompanied by planets; and even if they have such familes, there is no guarantee that intelligent beings will exist in their systems. Besides, it would be amazingly lucky if any astronomers there picked up our transmissions and replied to them straight away. Yet it is a measure of our changing attitude that the experiment has been considered worth making at all.

When we talk about "life", we have to confine ourselves to "life as we know it". Story-tellers delight in describing utterly alien creatures—made of pure gold, perhaps, and breathing carbon dioxide instead of oxygen. We cannot say that such creatures are impossible; our knowledge is still too slight. However, all the scientific evidence so far available indicates that life in the universe, wherever it may occur, will be essentially similar to that which we know on Earth. It may differ in form—beings of other races need not necessarily have one head and two arms each, for instance—but it will be made of the same materials. Until we have some definite evidence of alien life-forms, it is best to assume that such creatures do not exist.

SCIENCE NEWS

Going Down—With a Rotachute!

All the disadvantages of parachutes—time taken to open, lack of control during descent, intricate packing requirements, etc.—are eliminated in the Rotachute. This is a device consisting of two autogiro-type rotors mounted one above the other on a stout metal tube. A T-piece at the bottom of the tube provides a seat for the user and there is a safety strap as well to loop round the user's body. A steering handle acts on the rotor axes to tilt them, as required, to control the direction of descent. When not in use, the rotor blades fold down flat against the column and the seat-pieces slide up inside the column to make a convenient package.

Indestructible Transistors

Transistors—sub-miniature electronic components replacing conventional valves in many modern circuits—have now been developed to withstand shock tests of up to 1500 "g". That makes them virtually indestructible, even for use in missiles. Glass nuts and bolts are used in missiles, rockets, and other applications where parts are subject to extreme heat. They are machined from glass fibre (fibreglass) and look just like ordinary nuts and bolts, except for colour. Under really hot working conditions this material tends to vaporize slowly and in so doing provide its own cooling.

THE UMPIRE

IS

NOT

A

BOUNDARY!

by HYLTON CLEAVER

THE genius of Euclid defined a line as the distance between two points, having length without breadth. But so far there has been no genius in sport who can make up his mind as readily as Euclid about the functions of the white lines drawn to mark out our fields of play. The contradicting conclusions, to which sport's law-makers have come, are so astonishing that they would make Euclid give up in despair. A ball which pitches bang on the side-line in lawn tennis is, for example, *in* play. If, at Rugby, the ball passes through the air over the touch-line and, without pitching is blown back again, it is *out* of play. Yet a player can run up the field on the wrong side of the touch line, and still play the ball with his foot, providing the ball remains the right side of the line.

What decides victory in a running race? Many people think the winner is he who first breaks the tape; but it is not so. A tape, which blows about in the wind, is no means of judging at all—the finishing line must be drawn on the ground. The tape is only there to give the runner something to aim at in his final burst, and to assist the judges. In races between horses and boats we hear a lot about the winning post; but there can be no *one* winning post. There must surely be two, with an imaginary line between them, and in judging who has reached this line first we are greatly aided by the photo-finish camera. The horse wins by getting his nose in front, and a white line is even shown on the negative so that the exact position of the noses can be seen.

Many finishes of this type, especially speed tests in show-jumping, are judged by the breaking of an electric ray as the horses pass through it, thus stopping the clock instantly. This applies also to boat races, especially those abroad, which are nearly always judged by electric timing, and not by the stopwatch. A horse wins by a short head; a boat by getting its bows there first. There is no need for the complete crew or the complete horse to pass over the finishing line. The runner can get there with any part of his body above the waist, unless he falls headlong during the last stride! Then he must scramble on until every part of his frame has gone over the line.

Whether such lines as this should have any stipulated breadth is open to doubt. In squash and basketball it is laid down, in defiance of Euclid, that the lines should be two inches wide. The base line in lawn tennis can be four inches. Nothing is said about the width of the popping crease in cricket. It must be eight feet eight inches long and four feet from the stumps. It makes one wonder why someone with a sense of mischief has never chalked the line a whole foot wide! Then it would seem to be almost impossible to get the batsman stumped at all. But the laws clearly state that a batsman is "out of his ground" unless some part of his person, or bat, is grounded *within* the line of the popping crease. This means that if the batsman has his toe grounded *on* the line when the wicket-keeper stumps him, he is out.

Odd as many of these different interpretations of the white line seem, there is an excuse for *some* of them. The whole of the ball must pass right over the line at soccer before it is out of play and in touch; but it would not be right for this to be applied to a boundary at cricket. On many club grounds the boundary is not a line but a fence, and it is sufficient for the ball to hit this and rebound into play. Otherwise it counts six.

In some games there are no boundaries at all, notably lacrosse. In boxing, one man can be half out of the ring with his head through the ropes, but he is only regarded as out of play if he is unable to defend himself. He is not even knocked out if he pitches right out of the ring and lands in a spectator's lap, providing he gets back in time! If we were to accept Euclid's theory, the white line on the field of play would be as imaginary as the equator. The dividing line would then be no thicker than a stretched piece of cotton, and we should have no more trouble at Wimbledon between disgruntled players and linesmen. The ball would be on one side of the line or the other, but never *on* it.

One or two other laws on this matter are of interest. A Rugby goal-post is part of the goal-line, so theoretically you can score a try against it! You cannot draw a white line on water, so the only way to mark a course is by booms or buoys. If the boat hits these it is not put out of the race, in fact a craft has been known to slide between the buoys and finish up the wrong side of them, yet be declared the winner. The decision here is based on the fact that a boat's correct course is the quickest one to the finish providing it does not interfere with an opponent. By going outside the buoys a boat has gone the longest way round and so handicapped itself!

If flags or posts are used to denote the boundary on a cricket field, the space between them must be judged by an "imaginary line" linking them up. A ball can have passed over this and remain in play. A fielder in the deep can bend over backwards, jump high, and catch it without falling over the boundary himself. This is in direct opposition to the Rugby decree that once the ball has gone over it is out of play, even if blown back by the wind before it pitches. Incidentally, the

umpire is *not* a boundary, but the sight screen may be! It is not a boundary if the ball strikes any obstacles, such as trees, spectators, or chairs, within the playing area. As the batsman may be caught by a ball which rebounds off an "obstacle" he can conceivably hit the umpire on the head with the ball, which is subsequently caught, and so render himself *and* the official "out" with one stroke!

You can devise an interesting quiz among your friends on subjects such as these, providing you have all the answers. For instance, is a runner ruled out of the race if he steps over the inside line of the track? Does a racing boat have its bows on the starting line or its stern? But finally, and most important of all, why cannot the governing bodies of our different sports agree among themselves whether the thin white lines are in play or out?

SCIENCE NEWS

Fourteen Messages on One Tape Recorder

What happens if you drop a tape recorder? Most probably it breaks! But not a new, miniature model which has been developed for industrial use. Fitting into a case only four inches in diameter and three inches in height it could even be fired from a gun and still work. It is rated to take an impact shock of 500 times the force of gravity and survive acceleration up to 1500 "g". What is more, it can record fourteen different messages simultaneously!

Plastic Models Travel at 26,000 m.p.h.

A high-power hydrogen "gun" is used to fire plastic models at test speeds up to 26,000 miles per hour for research purposes. This is something like twenty times the speed a bullet leaves a rifle. Principle of the cartridge is that the breech end is sealed with a metal diaphragm and then charged with hydrogen gas. An electric spark instantaneously heats the hydrogen causing it to expand with explosion force, shatter the metal diaphragm and shoot the plastic projectile down the barrel.

Outboard Jet Motors

Even outboard motors are now jet propelled. New designs dispense with the propeller and use instead an internal pump to force out a jet of water for propulsion. Main advantage is no propeller to foul under-water obstructions of weed, and improved manoeuvrability. The first outboard motors, incidentally, were made way back in the late 1800's, and patented in France in 1864.

QUENTIN QUAYNE

Lord Peter Wimsey

"1066"

SHERLOCK HOLMES

Charlie Chan

SEXTON BLAKE

Perry Mason

LUDOVIC TRAVERS

Hercule Poirot

Inspector Maigret

SGT. CUFF

Roderick Alleyn

INSPECTOR FRENCH

RAFFLES

Father Brown

PAUL TEMPLE

SUPT. WILSON

FAMOUS DETECTIVES
OF FICTION

by

F. ADDINGTON SYMONDS

TALK of detectives and you may well think of Sherlock Holmes, or Sexton Blake, or the stars of television, Inspector Maigret or Perry Mason. But the earliest of all "whodunits" goes back more than 2,000 years, to the works of Herodotus and Virgil, and also the Jewish Apocrypha, all contain stories of crime and detection, complete with clues, red herrings and final *dénouement*. Sherlock Holmes himself, who first appeared in 1887 in *A Study in Scarlet*, is said to have been based on the famous Edinburgh surgeon, Dr. Joseph Bell; but his real prototype was M. Auguste Dupin, featured by Edgar Allan Poe in his trilogy, *Murders in the Rue Morgue*, *The Purloined Letter*, and *The Mystery of Marie Roget*. Dupin, who made his bow in 1846, was the father of a long line of eccentric detectives of fiction and was followed by the more sedate Sgt. Cuff, in Wilkie Collins' *The Woman in White* [1860] and *The Moonstone* [1868], the latter being, in the opinion of many, one of the greatest detective stories of all time. Then there was old Ebenezer Gryce, the "hero" of *The Leavenworth Case* [1883] and other novels by the American writer, Anna Katharine Green, whose works were best sellers in their day.

Holmes undoubtedly set the fashion and, though he was followed by a spate of others, he remains the model of them all. Oddly enough, his creator, Sir Arthur Conan Doyle, had little patience with him! "I've always felt," he is reported to have said, "that Holmes is hardly human, that he is really nothing but a calculating machine." But his millions of readers all over the world have decided otherwise. Many, indeed, believed that he was a living person, and today, more than 70 years since his first appearance, Holmes is as popular as ever. Most of his many successors are now almost forgotten, though not always deservedly so. Among them were Martin Hewitt, the barrister-turned-detective, whose adventures were chronicled by the Victorian novelist, Arthur Morrison; the truculent, matter-of-fact Professor Auguste S.F.X. Van Dusen, known as "the Thinking Machine", by Jacques Futrelle; Fleming Stone, featured in many fine stories by the American writer, Carolyn Wells; the Baroness Orczy's nameless Old Man in the Corner, who solved problems while sitting in a teashop, tying knots in a piece of string; Hamilton Cleek, "the Man with the Forty Faces", by T. W. Hanshew; and the once immensely popular Charlie Chan, who first appeared in Earl Derr Biggers' *Seven Keys to Baldplate* [1913] and afterwards in a score of films. Others include Ernest Bramah's blind detective, Max Carrados; Uncle Abner, the rugged "Master of Mystery" created by Melville Davisson Post; and the Urbane "Q.-Q.", (Quentin Quayne) about whom F. Britten Austin wrote a series of stories some forty years ago in the *Strand Magazine*.

"The Yawning Detectives"

The most outstanding figure in the period immediately following the appearance of Sherlock Holmes was tall and handsome Dr. John Thorndyke, introduced by R. Austin Freeman in the first decade of this century. Thorndyke, with his microscope and test tubes, was the original "scientific" detective. Some of his fictional methods were actually put into practice by real police and he himself was a great character, undeserving of the comparative oblivion into which he has now fallen. The names of more recent and contemporary fiction detectives are virtually legion and one of the earlier of these was M. Hanaud, of the Paris *Sûreté*, who made his first appearance before the First World War in A. E. W. Mason's *At the Villa Rose*. Hanaud's peacock vanity and his air of intellectual aloofness sometimes verged on the comic, but he was in the classic tradition and his cases made fascinating reading.

Still remembered is the pseudo-academic Philo Vance, featured in *The Benson Murder Case* and other novels by the American, S. S. van

Dine. Vance was described by his author as being "an art collector, a fine pianist, and a profound student of aesthetics", whose interest in crime was a kind of side-line. His opposite number in this country is Lord Peter Wimsey, the aristocratic dilettante with a pretty taste in wines and haberdashery, so cleverly portrayed by Dorothy L. Sayers in a series of still popular stories. Linked with these two characters is Reggie Fortune, the frivolous, semi-official sleuth created by H. C. Bailey, all three having been described by one writer as the "yawning detectives", doubtless because both their authors wrote stories which were noted as much for their facetiousness as for the more serious plots on which they were based.

Another of the eccentrics is Father Brown, the whimsical little priest detective created by G. K. Chesterton. Father Brown is unique—quite the most original of all fiction detectives. In fact, some critics insist that he is not a detective at all but one who is interested more in sinners than criminals. His problems are often weird and grotesque, his methods more intuitional than analytical; but his individuality puts him in a class apart. High on the list of contemporaries is Ellery Queen, still going strong after more than thirty years. He—or, rather, they, being father and son—are the joint product of Frederick Dannay and Manfred B. Lee, two American writers who combine the Holmes tradition with the most bizarre, and often very complicated, plots. Similarly fantastic are the stories featuring Sir Henry Merivale ("H.M.") and Dr. Gideon Fell, by Carter Dickson and John Dickson Carr respectively, though both writers are one and the same. These two swashbuckling firebrands are much alike in character and mannerisms and some readers find them wearisome, though their cases are invariably highly original.

Other popular modern detectives include Erle Stanley Gardner's American lawyer, Perry Mason; Christopher Bush's horn-rimmed Ludovic Travers; Margery Allingham's Albert Campion; Edmund Crispin's whimsical Gervase Fen, and Harvey Tuke, the "hero" of a series of clever stories by Douglas Browne. Unquestionably the greatest of them all is Agatha Christie's little Belgian, Hercule Poirot, with his egg-shaped head, his waxed moustache, and his "little grey cells". Ever since his first appearance, many years ago, in *The Mysterious Affair at Styles*, he has captured the imagination of countless readers with his comic flamboyance, his conceit—"I am probably the greatest detective in the world"—and his absurd yet lovable mannerisms.

Latterly, however, the trend has been more towards the official detective, the "man from Scotland Yard," though he made an early appearance as long ago as 1921 with the creation of Inspector French in Freeman Wills Crofts' masterpiece, *The Cask*. French is a "natural"—an ordinary man who makes no pretensions to infallibility but "worries things out", often making mistakes. Modelled upon him was Supt. Wilson, in *Poison in a Garden Suburb* and other very competent stories by G. D. H. and M. Cole. Others include Michael Innes' Inspector John Appleby, E. C. R. Lorac's Chief Inspector Macdonald, the New Zealand author, Ngaio Marsh, and her increasingly popular Roderick Alleyn, and the internationally famous Inspector Maigret who appears in countless stories written by Georges Simenon.

These *official* detectives are more human and approximate more nearly to real life, which doubtless accounts for their greater popularity in our essentially realistic times. One of them at least is as remarkable for his failures as for his successes—the amusing and lovable M. Pinaud, who appears in *The Two Impostors* and other novels by the latest, very clever addition to the ranks of detective-story writers, Pierre Audemars. But Pinaud is not, perhaps, so much a detective in the accepted sense as a student of human nature, a *comic* who combines an unconscious wit with a rare compassion and a most doughty conscience!

Thriller 'Tecs

All these and many more appear only in *whodunits*—stories of pure detection as distinct from the *thriller*, which is more concerned with action and adventure and has its own gallery of colourful and picturesque heroes, ranging from Arsene Lupin to Raffles and culminating in their natural descendants, the Saint, the Toff, Lemmy Caution, Norman Conquest and Paul Temple—though the latter is, of course, a *legitimate* crime investigator. So, also, is Sexton Blake, whose name was such a household word in Britain that it was almost inevitably coupled with that of Sherlock Holmes. Blake, first invented more than fifty years ago by a writer named Harry Blyth, was obviously modelled on Holmes, though the two had little in common beyond their physical appearance, and the fact that both had their headquarters in Baker Street. (Now the 1961 Blake has forsaken that famous thoroughfare for more chromium-plated premises in Berkeley Square!)

Sexton Blake appeared in innumerable stories by an army of chiefly anonymous authors, with translations into most European languages; his adventures have been portrayed on stage and screen; and his fans banded themselves into a *Sexton Blake Circle* which, like the *Baker*

Street Irregulars (supporters of Sherlock Holmes) meet regularly for lectures, readings, and discussions. Collectors vie with each other in building up libraries of his stories and astonishingly high prices are cheerfully paid for "rare editions". Blake's opposite number in America was the once famous Nick Carter (whose adventures were also translated into foreign languages) and he has had many imitators in the same field: Nelson Lee, Dixon Hawke, Ferrers Locke, "Panther" Grayle and others. Is it mere coincidence that so many of the names of these fictional detectives bear such a syllabic resemblance to each other? The first names, you will have noticed, invariably consist of two syllables, the second of only one. But it was Sherlock Holmes who started it!

The pageant of the fiction detectives is a long and fascinating one, crowded with an almost limitless variety of characters, and only a bird's eye view of it has been possible here. But these names testify to the immense popularity of the detective story. The demand for this class of fiction today is greater than ever.

B.O.P readers will be quick to point out that Boy's Own Paper *has its own famous detective of fiction in Superintendent Slade, created by Leonard Gribble. Since he first made his appearance in 1950, Slade has had five series of cases and stories in B.O.P as well as his famous Ten Minute Mysteries. Some have been included in this and previous volumes of the* Companion *series.—Editor.*

"*Guess who?*"

TRAINSPOTTERS' CROSSWORD

Set by GORDON DOUGLAS

Clues Across

1. The beacon of railway safety (6) . . .
4. . . . that's green when the line is this (5).
7. This cap goes to boot (3).
8. Disconnect—two coaches, perhaps (8).
9. What it costs to make a come-back? (6, 4).
11. How to address a man you see nightly (3).
12. Admiration in a welcome (3).
15. Doesn't spud bring us to a violent halt? (6, 4).
16. Fast bowlers with a drop of tea inside? You don't often see them bowling along Southern electric lines (8).
17. You'll find the lot at the end of the booking hall (3).
18. Clerical dignitary who sounds like a London Street station (5).
19. Sharp switches on the line (6).

Clues Down

1. On which the SO soccer special runs (8).
2. The stock of this famous old company was brown and cream (5, 12).
3. An inner surface—or laying track? (6).
4. The kind of music for people in good voice (6).
5. This moves quickly along the right lines (7, 5).
6. Cruet is a source of regret (3).
10. Wrestles with some crane claws (8).
13. This fellow will never get even (3, 3).
14. Put ear to the line and demolish it (4, 2).
16. A little pouch to start putting saccharine in? (3).

(Solution on page 191)

DON'T HIT THE BALL HARD!

D. J. ("DAI") REES, *the famous Ryder Cup captain and West Herts professional, gives hints to young golfers.*

ASSUMING that you have watched players in an important tournament or championship, you will at once agree with me when I say that golf is the easiest game in the world! It is, *if* you master the rudiments of the game, and are prepared to work hard to put them into practice. If you approach it with a "don't care" attitude and just hit the ball as hard as you can, it can be the most heart-breaking game of all.

To take last things first, I suppose that the most common fallacy among young beginners is the belief that the harder one hits the ball the farther it will travel. There is no greater fallacy. Let us get this right: *don't try to hit the ball hard.* Golf is full of apparent contradictions. Stand as you would to hook a bowler to the boundary and probably the ball will sail out to the right: certainly not to the left. If you are inclined to "top" your shots you may decide to stand in front, or ahead, of the ball. The more effective cure is to stand farther behind it. A deep-faced club may look the most likely implement to get the ball into the air, but it is nothing like so effective as a narrow, or, as we call it, shallow-faced club.

It seems all wrong I know, but as I have already told you, the game is full of contradictions. That is why, when you watch great golfers playing, it looks so easy. They have been, and are, working hard at the game. I cannot go into technical explanations in this short article; I doubt whether you would be interested if I did. I hope to set you on the right road, however, to good golf which, of course, means enjoyable golf. You cannot expect to enjoy the game if you spend most of the time looking for your ball in the rough!

So let us get down to it with a few brief hints, which I hope may help you to get as much fun out of the game as I do—believe it or not, I enjoy playing golf even though it is my living. I will assume that you have never played golf or that occasionally during holidays you have borrowed a few clubs and played what you call golf. If you want to enjoy the game, go to a good teacher and learn the elementary principles of the stance, the grip, and the swing. Do not go on playing in the hope that you will improve. That is extremely unlikely, unless you accidentally use the proper methods of hitting the ball and controlling your swing. It is far more probable that you are making one of the many common errors; either your grip is wrong—your right hand is in its apparently natural, but wrong position under the shaft, with your knuckles pointing to the ground; or your stance, with the ball mid-way between the feet, as you may have seen in photographs, is making it difficult for you to strike your drives properly.

An experienced professional can see these things at once. He can tell at a glance whether you are standing correctly, making the proper use of your hands and wrists, using your arms properly and employing the leg and waist muscles to the best advantage. He can at least put you on the right road in three or four lessons. But you cannot expect to play golf after this scant tuition; you must first spend a lot of time at practice. You will find the practice invaluable later.

Do not go on the course after a few lessons and tell your friends all about your proficiency—it might make you look stupid—but go into the practice nets, or some part of the course where you can try out the lessons you have learned. Take a club and keep on hitting shots with it until you feel confident of hitting the ball in the approximately correct direction without fear of missing it. Fear is the enemy of good golf—even to champions! If you go out on the course thinking "I might miss this shot," you *will* miss it. It is useless "hitting and hoping"; it will get you nowhere. So be sure you have started right and then persevere by mastering the instructions, confusing though they may appear, of your tutor. I do not want to discourage courtesy, but try to forget the "good advice" of other golfers and stick to your tutor.

Study the Boys' Championship

Now let us suppose that you have played golf, in fact you may think of competing in the Boys' Championship—a very good thing to do, if only that it will teach you that your golf is not quite so good as you thought it to be. You may have discussed the theories of the game with other players and you may think you know all about them. Believe me, you do not. I do not wish to discourage you, but I assure you that although I have been in the game for over thirty years I am still learning. I have seen young competitors in tournaments who will never improve; in fact, as they lose some of the suppleness of youth their golf will almost certainly deteriorate unless they change their methods. So,

79

if you play a reasonable game now, make sure that your methods are right. If possible watch leading amateur and professional golfers, those whom one expects to win championships and tournaments. I know that boys are great imitators. I used to try to copy some of the great golfers —after my father had taught me how to play.

It is useless watching great golfers unless you know what to look for. Stand facing the player. Watch where he places his feet and note how he grips the club. There are several methods of gripping the club, and with rare exceptions all these different methods—the overlap, the interlock, and the palm or V-grips—are all correct. You must discover, with the aid of your teacher, which suits you best. Now comes the most difficult part of watching. Try to see how the player starts his swing. It looks as though the initial movement may come from the feet and legs— certainly not from the hands. Then watch his body movement as the club is taken back. You will notice that his left side has not moved from the vertical, but that his body seems to have moved round as though it is a door with hinges on its left side. None of that swaying which seems to be necessary when you are trying to hit an extra long one!

You will have a quick eye if you can see the actual contact between the club-head and the ball; but you can watch the hands and feet of the player at the moment of impact and immediately afterwards. Do not watch the ball: watch the player. If there is a crowd watching, you will not disturb him if you stand still immediately behind. Get in this position and you will obtain a good view of the arc of the swing. By watching good golfers you will realize that they all employ similar methods, though at first glance they appear to be different. Some swing faster than others, some swings are longer than others, but the same guiding principles are always observed. Try to copy the good golfer you admire. Try out your swing in your bedroom in front of the wardrobe mirror. Take your club back half-way. Does that look anything like the expert? Now take it back farther. What does it look like at the top of the swing? Now strike an imaginary ball and try to stop the club at the point of impact; then follow through and look at yourself. You will see that it looks different.

Do not be discouraged because there is so much to learn in golf. Any good professional golfer will help you, not only because he is paid to teach, but because he loves the game and wants to help. But you must help yourself. Make sure your methods are right and then practise, practise, practise! We professionals have to practise hard all the time, so why not the beginner? There is no need to make a misery of practice.

You can get quite a lot of fun out of it. Aim at a mark you can reach and get down to it until you have gained complete confidence with that club; then do the same with another and another. Get to know your clubs and think of them as friends. If you cannot get on friendly terms with a club, discard it. If you are playing it correctly, an unfriendly club will never be of any use to you. It may be a perfect club but unsuitable.

Seek Expert Advice when Buying Clubs

Choose your clubs with the aid of a professional. He will not try to sell you unsuitable clubs. Never buy clubs carelessly so that you may have to model your golf to them. Buy clubs which will suit your own style. Having told you what a lot of hard work you must do to become a good golfer, let me add a word of encouragement and warning. Golf is, as I have said, the easiest game in the world. *You* can play it well if you try. There is nothing to hitting the ball if you start in the right way; but on no account allow golf to take up *all* your leisure time. Just practise hard when you feel like it. But do not take your golf tuition so seriously that the game becomes a task. Rather go out and play a round if you feel that this is the way to learn.

I am not sure that I should approve, but I would much rather you enjoyed your golf than anything else. It is a grand game, but a bad master. I enjoy playing. If *you* do not, my advice is do not *try* to play it. In conclusion, here are a few useful hints:

Make sure that your stance, your grip, and your swing are correct. Ask an expert about these things. Do not be discouraged by early failures to accomplish the shots which you think you ought to be able to play. Even champions miss a shot occasionally!

If there is any one shot you *cannot* play, and you are sure that your methods are right, go out and practise that shot. You will discover that it is easy after a while. Do not try to hit the ball hard. Swing the club, and timing will become a habit. Good timing means longer shots.

There is no easy way to golf proficiency. For most of us it means study and practice. But do not try to copy me or other golfers. Let your tutor form your style and he will tell you that we all follow the same principles. Golf is an individual game and if you start in the right way you naturally develop a good style. Above all, do not make golf a drudgery. If you cannot enjoy practice—well, just go on hitting and missing! You will still enjoy the game immensely!

Spot the Vintage Makes

⑥

⑦

⑧

⑨

⑩

⑪

⑫

(Solution page
192)

HIDDEN SPORTS

BELOW are some phrases, each one of which gives the clue to the name of a well-known sport. The answer may be phonetic, an outrageous pun, or even straightforward! Figures following the clue indicate the number of words in the sport-name. Here is an example of what you may expect:—*Clue*. A single bullet—makes mistakes. *Answer*. Rounders (Round-errs). Now see how many you can find.

1. A wooden case—Chant (1).

2. Display—A flea's speciality (2).

3. A mat—An insect (1).

4. *Aqua-pura*—A famous traveller of old (2).

5. A muscular pain—Half a well-known volcano (1).

6. What is an even number? (1).

7. A short stocking—A mongrel dog (1).

8. Crammed full—nothing left out—A quiet "break" with a fish (3).

9. Century—9 feet—A quick run (3).

10. Foundation—A dancing party (1).

11. Doctor tells you to say this—A fruit (1).

12. A "reject" of a famous brand of chinaware (1).

(*Answers on page 192*)

KEEP YOUR RABBITS IN COLONIES

by

C. F. SNOW

WHEN we speak of keeping rabbits in colonies, we mean a run in which several rabbits live together. The groups of rabbits chosen for colonies are usually of the same age and of the same sex. Colonies may be either indoors or, during summer months, out of doors. A small shed or poultry house, or a lean-to shed, will make an excellent indoor colony run for a group of rabbits. Young rabbits usually do very well when kept in colonies, because it gives them ample room for exercise. If you want your rabbits to produce prime pelts, however, they must not be left in colonies after they are five months old. If there are several rabbits together, there is always a risk of the pelt becoming soiled or damaged, so pelt rabbits must have a hutch to themselves.

When deciding how many youngsters to put into a colony, allow a minimum floor space of 2 square feet for each rabbit. If you have a large shed, it would be better to divide it up into separate pens. Partitions can be made with wire netting of 1-inch mesh, mounted on wood framing of 2 by 1 inch. The partitions should be about 3 feet high to keep the rabbits from jumping over them. It is not advisable to have more than about twenty rabbits in one colony pen, even if there is plenty of floor

85

space for them. The reason for this is that rabbits are rather easily frightened and the more rabbits there are together, the greater the panic they create among themselves. If they are startled by an unusual noise, or by a stranger approaching them, they may stampede in a wild rush to one end of the pen. If too large a number of rabbits are involved in this, some may be badly injured.

When making rabbit colonies in a shed or outbuilding, make sure that it is vermin-proof, otherwise you may lose some of your rabbits. Also make sure that there are no floor draughts. Rabbits can stand cold, but they cannot stand draughts or damp conditions. A wood floor is best for colony pens, but concrete floors can be successful, provided plenty of litter is used. Whatever type of floor is used, it is essential to have plenty of litter. The best floor covering is a good layer of sawdust, about $\frac{1}{8}$ inch thick, covered with straw or rough hay. On a concrete floor the layer of straw will need to be thicker than on a wooden one to provide extra warmth. If 2 square feet or more of floor space is allowed, it will only be necessary to clean out the pens about once a week.

Fix hay racks on the side of the pens, so that hay and greenstuff does not come into contact with the floor. Mash should be fed in troughs, and drinking water should be provided in heavy vessels that cannot be tipped over. See that the hay racks and food troughs are big enough to accommodate all the rabbits at once, otherwise the weaker ones will be pushed aside and may not get enough to eat.

A litter of weaned youngsters can be put together in a colony, or a colony of young does or of young bucks can be made up from different litters. Young bucks are usually taken from the colonies of bucks and does by the time they are about four months old. If a colony of young bucks have been together since weaning and there are no does nearby to disturb them, they will usually live in peace for several months. The usual practice is to get rid of surplus bucks at about four-and-a-half to five months old, and to house any bucks kept for breeding or showing separately after that age. Does may be left together in a colony for any length of time, and rarely fight. Never try to make up a colony of adult bucks, otherwise there will certainly be a great deal of fighting, and the rabbits may be seriously injured.

The advantage of the colony system is that colony runs are cheaper to make than hutches, and colonies are labour-saving, too. Feeding is quicker, and the cleaning of pens is quite simple and quick. Rabbits in inside colonies should receive the same amount of food as those in hutches, and it will usually be found that these rabbits grow quickly and develop well, probably due to the extra space which gives them room for exercise.

Use a Supplementary Hutch

During the spring and summer and for part of the autumn, rabbits can be housed out of doors in Morant hutches. Morant hutches are movable hutches or pens, which will hold up to a dozen rabbits. These hutches have wire netting floors of 2-inch mesh, and are moved daily to a fresh patch of grass, so that the rabbits can eat the green-food thus provided for them. With this method there is no cleaning out necessary, neither is there any need to gather greenfood for the rabbits if the grass on which they are placed is a good, rich mixture. If, however, the grass is sparse, or of poor quality, they will need extra greenfood. Rabbits in Morant hutches will also need some hay and a little mash, oats, or bran several times a week. They should not be expected to get all the food they need from the grazing provided, but they will get a big part of it, and so help you.

There are several possible designs for Morant hutches, but the underlying principle is the same. The hutch must be light, so that it can be moved easily from one place to another, and it must be fitted with handles for lifting. One part of the hutch must be covered, both as a protection against rain and cold winds, and also against strong sunlight in hot weather. If the covered-in part has floor boards fitted to it, slightly raised from the ground, this serves as sleeping quarters for the rabbits. Some breeders prefer to have the whole floor of wire netting, and to put raised shelves for sleeping round the sides of the covered-in part. Others provide a large box for sleeping quarters. Any of these is satisfactory, but the rabbits should not be allowed to sleep on the wire-netting floor.

The hutch itself should be about 7 feet long, 2 feet wide, and rise to an apex about 3 feet high. The covered part of the hutch should be about 3 feet long. The hutch should open completely at either end, for ease in getting rabbits in and out and for cleaning the sleeping compartment if it has a solid floor. One-inch mesh netting is suitable for the sides of the hutch, and 2-inch mesh for the floors. Young rabbits can be put into Morant hutches at about eight weeks old, that is about a week or ten days after weaning. It is best to choose a mild, sunny day before putting them into outdoor colonies. If the youngsters are to provide good pelts later on, see that the hutches are never exposed to the full glare of the sun, otherwise the rabbits' coats will become faded.

RUNAWAY ROCKET

by

H. B. GREGORY

JIM BALLANTYNE stood in the shadow of the giant rocket, hands stuck in the pockets of his faded jeans, freckled face upturned, as, with blue eyes squinting in the glare, he gazed up at the shining hull towering into the blazing sky. Very soon now this steel monster would roar up into the blue, belching fire, and the first manned flight to the Moon would begin. But, Jim reflected sadly, he would not be on board: worse, he would not even be here to see the launching, for the holidays would be over, and he would be back at school in Port Augusta.

The boy kicked angrily at the foot of the gantry against which he stood, hurting himself more than the steel, for he was wearing only canvas shoes. What was the use, he thought, of having James Ballantyne, D.Sc., Director of the Anglo-Australian Moon Rocket Project, for a father if he couldn't even see the start of that historic voyage!

Dr. Ballantyne smiled as he looked down from the platform near the top of the gantry, and saw that frustrated kick. He knew quite well what was eating his son, and had already decided to arrange for him to stay for the launching.

"Come up, Jim!" he shouted.

Jim was only rarely allowed inside the control cabin of the rocket. He wasted no time waiting for the lift which was bringing the engineers down to ground level, but began climbing the vertical steel ladder. The lift passed before he was half-way up, and seeing that one of the passengers was Tom Fleming, whom he knew to be going on leave today, Jim shouted: "Cheerio, Mr. Fleming; have a good holiday!"

Fleming had not time to reply, but raised a hand in acknowledgement. He was a lean, dark man, with few friends, but he had always been ready to talk to Jim, and to answer his endless questions about the ship. The other men grinned as the lift shot downwards. Jim was generally popular with the Project team, and not only because his father was Director.

When Jim reached the platform, his father had already gone back through the entry port into the rocket, and the boy followed him through the air-lock into the cramped cabin where, facing the control panel, glittering with instruments, stood the three padded chair-couches in which the crew would be strapped for take-off.

Jim was a keen science student himself, bent on following in his famous father's footsteps, so he was able to understand the function of most of the control mechanisms. To his great delight, he was again allowed to sit in the pilot's chair, and to buckle the safety harness around him. It didn't fit very closely since, although tough and wiry, he was small for his fourteen years, but, as he sat there with the instruments and control gear arrayed before him, he could almost imagine he was really flying through space towards the Moon. He closed his eyes, and sighed deeply.

"I know just how you feel. What wouldn't I give to be going with

89

them too?" said Dr. Ballantyne. He ran his lean, sensitive fingers through his thick, grey hair, unruly as his son's own sandy thatch. "But I'm too old, and you're too young. Cheer up, son! You'll be just right for the first Mars run!"

"That won't be the same, dad. This is the first ever."

There was no answer to that, so Dr. Ballantyne went on to explain the controls of the radio equipment, which had been completed since Jim's last visit. Presently a bell rang, and a red light glowed on the instrument panel.

The Director stood up: "Come on, Jim. We must get out now. They're going to begin filling the tanks."

"Already, dad?"

"Yes. We want to give the motors a trial run tomorrow. Low speed, of course. We're not ready to go, yet."

"What's still to be done, dad?"

"Not much here, except for testing. We've still to plot the final course, and set it up on the auto-pilot, but the ship herself is just about ready to go."

When Jim and his father reached the ground, two big red tankers were being backed up to the base of the rocket, and, from a safe distance, they watched the fuelling team, looking like space-men themselves in their protective suits and helmets, connect the pipe lines.

"Is it so dangerous?" Jim asked.

"Liquid fluorine and hydrogen? Just about the most violent combination possible, apart from plutonium and uranium ·235, but the most successful rocket fuel yet, since we found the right material to line the tanks."

When sufficient fuel for the motor tests had been pumped into the rocket and the tankers had gone, Dr. Ballantyne and his son climbed into the waiting Land Rover. Jim was allowed to drive on the pathways within the perimeter fence, since these were not public roads, but they stopped at the gate to change places. Dr. Ballantyne spoke to the uniformed security guard on duty.

"Who's on the gate tonight?" he asked

"Pearson and Grant, sir."

"Grant? He's new, isn't he?"

"Too right, sir. But Pearson's an old hand. He'll show him the drill."

"Good. From now on, no one is to be allowed into the compound after dark. And by day, only those with a pass signed personally by me."

"Right, sir. I'll pass it on."

90

Dr. Ballantyne climbed back into the Land Rover, and the guard swung back the heavy gate to let them through.

"Expecting trouble, dad?"

"Not particularly. But there are a lot of people who would very much like to see this project fail, Jim."

A few minutes' drive took them to the bungalows occupied by the Project personnel. Dr. Ballantyne, although a widower, had one to himself, and here Jim stayed with his father during his holidays from school. After their evening meal, leaving his father at work on the daily progress report, Jim caught the bus into Woomera to see an old Western film. On his way home after the show, Jim decided to visit the rocket site before going to bed. It had been very hot in the cinema and the rattle of six-shooters had given him a slight headache. It was very pleasant swinging along in the cool night air, under a moonless sky bright with stars, after he left the bus.

He had done this before, and knew the guards welcomed a break in their lonely vigil, but, as he drew near the gate, Jim was hoping that Pearson would be on duty, and not Grant, whom he did not know. To his surprise, neither was in sight. One of them was supposed to be there at all times. Jim crept up to the small wicket beside the main gate, silent on his rubber soles, and peered through the bars. As he rested his weight on it, the gate moved. It was open.

Jim's mouth went dry. What should he do? He mustn't panic. Perhaps it was just carelessness. He must investigate further before raising the alarm. He slipped through the gate, and stole silently up to the lighted window of the guard-room. What he saw there made him reel with horror.

Pearson lay huddled on the floor, his eyes staring, his head in a pool of blood. Over him, wiping the butt of a revolver, stood another man in uniform, who must be Grant. Worst of all, the third man, facing the window, was Tom Fleming, the engineer who had gone on leave that afternoon, and who should have been well on his way to his home in Sydney by now. Stepping cautiously back from the window, Jim thought furiously. Should he make a dash for his father's bungalow? It was over a mile away, and long before he could get help, whatever sabotage these traitors planned might have been done. No, he must go on, towards the rocket itself, and either telephone from the control tower, or set off the siren on the workshop roof. Without wasting another moment he began to run.

Three minutes later he was frantically stumbling from door to door

91

of the workshops and control tower, and finding them all securely locked. Fool! he told himself bitterly. Why didn't you think of that?

As he stood irresolute, blood pounding in his ears, his eye caught the flash of a torch, between him and the gate. Whatever he was going to do must be done quickly. He turned and ran on, towards the launching platform, three hundred yards away. Before him, gleaming faintly in the starlight, the slender bulk of the rocket loomed against the sky. Somehow he must save it! He pounded grimly on.

His breath was sobbing in his throat as he reached the foot of the gantry and leapt at the ladder, knowing that the power would be cut off from the lift. Hand over hand he hauled himself painfully upwards. Half-way up his foot slipped and he almost fell, clinging trembling to the steel rungs, his hands slippery with sweat. He forced himself to wait until his breathing steadied a little, then went on more cautiously.

As he crawled panting on to the platform, the beam of a powerful torch leapt at him from below, and a shot rang out, the bullet hitting the steel beside him and whining away into the night. Jim staggered to the entry port, and tugged at the sunken lever. The massive door swung open, allowing him to slip inside, then thudded back on to its rubber seating. He spun the wheel which sealed it fast and sank exhausted on the floor of the air-lock. A second bullet splashed on the outer skin of the rocket.

Some minutes later, the lock clicked as someone outside tried to open it, but Jim grinned in the darkness, knowing that, once it was sealed from within, the door could not be opened without the emergency key, which never left his father's possession. The ship was safe now, and so was he. All he had to do was to wait for daylight and rescue, if indeed the shooting had not already given the alarm. When he had recovered somewhat, Jim got to his feet, and felt his way into the cabin. It was pitch dark, but he groped for the pilot's chair, and sank gratefully into its padding. Now that no more effort was needed, he felt weak as a kitten. Soon he was asleep.

He was awakened by the sudden glare of the cabin lights, shining full on his face. He sat up, bewildered, rubbing his eyes, and stared aghast at the control panel. The red lever of the fluorine pump was moving over, as if grasped by an invisible hand. Underneath his feet the steel deck began to vibrate. Then he understood. The saboteurs had broken into the control tower, and were operating the remote controls, which had been connected by cable for tomorrow's test. But why only fluorine? The jets would not fire without hydrogen as well.

An icy chill swept over Jim as he guessed the fiendish plan. Tons of liquid fluorine would gush from the jets into the blast tunnel beneath the ship and lie there, boiling, until the hydrogen pumps were started. Then would follow a frightful explosion, less only than that of an atom bomb, and the ship would be instantly destroyed.

He grabbed the red lever, and tried frantically to push it back, but it was useless. His small strength was nothing to the electromagnets holding it. He let go, and stood for an instant, trembling in every limb. One desperate remedy alone remained. Could he remember the firing sequence? He drew a deep breath, and then, as calmly as he could, threw the switches over: oxygen, gyro-motors, auto-pilot, and, lastly, the blue lever of the hydrogen pump.

With a mighty roar, the main jets fired at full throttle, and Jim was flung back into his seat as the deck leapt beneath his feet. His weight grew and grew as the enormous acceleration crushed him mercilessly into the padding, and held him helpless, while the rocket hurtled towards the stars.

*　　*　　*

When the last bus from Woomera had arrived, and Jim had not returned, Dr. Ballantyne got out the Land Rover, and drove to the Project site, expecting to find his son at the gate, as on previous occasions. To his anger and dismay, there was no guard on duty, and the wicket was open. He went through, and stormed into the guardroom, almost falling over Pearson's body. The Director at once telephoned for help, and, taking a revolver, opened the main gate and drove towards the control tower, where he could see a light.

He was scarcely half-way there when the whole area was lit by a great gush of flame from the base of the rocket, and the huge ship rose into the air. Paralysed, Dr. Ballantyne stared at what he thought to be the ruin of all his work, expecting at any moment to see the rocket explode in mid-air, or dive down to destruction, but, incredibly, it went on climbing up into the night sky, veering slightly towards the northeast, dwindled to a red spark amidst the stars, and at last vanished.

His next thought was for Jim, who, he guessed, had somehow fallen foul of the saboteurs, and he drove furiously on to the control tower, leapt out, and raced up the stairs, revolver in hand. There he found Fleming about to demolish the equipment with a fireman's axe. The renegade engineer turned, his dark features twisting in a stupid grin, and leapt at the Director, swinging his axe. Dr. Ballantyne shot him dead.

At this moment the squad car arrived, and, after a brief search, the charred body of the traitor Grant was found, near the launching platform. He had been caught by the blast when the rocket took off unexpectedly. A further intensive search failed to reveal any trace of Jim, and an awful suspicion as to his son's possible fate began to take shape in Dr. Ballantyne's mind. It was useless to attempt even to track the rocket, much less to control it, unless its own transmitter was radiating, since the connections which had been made to the tower for the motor tests were temporary cable hook-ups, and had parted the instant the rocket lifted.

There was nothing to be done but to inform all listening posts and tracking stations throughout the world, and hope for a miracle. A lesser man might well have given way to despair, but Dr. Ballantyne had not been appointed Director for nothing. Within half an hour, all personnel had been brought to the site, and the whole area, under the glare of floodlights was a scene of intense, but highly organized activity.

One team was repairing the gantry, which had been slightly damaged by the unexpected launching; another was tuning up the telemetering and remote control gear; while in the tower itself the radio operators sat glued to their equipment, headphones on, eyes fixed on the flickering screens of cathode-ray tubes, as on the roof above, the great paraboloid of the radio telescope swung slowly round, scanning every quarter of the sky.

In the same room, Dr. Ballantyne, his face a rigid mask, sat at his desk, in direct communication with Jodrell Bank in far-off Manchester, where the giant radio telescope was already scanning the wintry sky on the other side of the globe.

* * *

When his senses returned, Jim found himself floating a few feet above the pilot's chair. The lights still shone on the control panel, the clock showing that he had been unconscious for only half an hour. All was so quiet and still that the boy wondered if he were dreaming. He tried to reach the seat below—or was it above?—but the movement only sent him sailing up—or was it down?—to the steel roof. His head swam, and he felt suddenly sick. So this was the much-discussed weightlessness of space flight! He wasn't sure he liked it very much. Very cautiously he pushed gently on the roof, and sailed back to the chair, grabbing the arms. He wriggled round into the seat, and quickly strapped himself in. That was a lot better! He leaned forward, and studied the instruments.

The needle of the altimeter was steady at a height of 1,075 miles. The relative speed indicator showed 15,800 m.p.h. By the greatest good fortune, the rocket had reached orbital velocity before the motors stopped. For the moment he was safe, but—was any fuel left? With his heart in his mouth, Jim switched on the gauges.

Two tanks only were full, one of fluorine, the other of hydrogen. The rest were empty. How many had been filled at the outset he had no idea, but it seemed a fairly safe guess that only one pair had been connected for the test. In that case, half the fuel was gone. There should be just enough to get him back to earth. Jim knew he could not hope to pilot the rocket himself. His only chance was to make radio contact with the control tower at Woomera—assuming that the saboteurs had not succeeded in wrecking the delicate equipment there, as they would undoubtedly try to do.

He switched on the transmitter, and, when it had warmed up, began to speak into the microphone: "Moon rocket calling Woomera! Moon rocket calling Woomera! Come in, please, Woomera."

He switched to receive, but only the meaningless sounds of static came from the loudspeaker. Again and again he tried, but there was no answer. Terror and a great loneliness began to grow in him. Had the saboteurs succeeded then, and was this beloved ship destined to become his coffin, swinging round and round the earth for ever, like a tiny moon?

Round the earth? Why hadn't he thought of that before? Quickly he unbuckled his harness, and cautiously floated to one of the viewing ports. He unscrewed the safety cover, and peered through the thick quartz out into the void. He caught his breath at the amazing sight.

The whole enormous globe of the earth hung before him, filling the sky, lit by the sun from in front of the rocket. Much of the surface was hidden by dazzling white cloud, but large areas of dark blue sea were visible, and, immediately below, the greens and browns of a great land mass, which he recognized, after a time, as the southern part of North America. Australia was, of course, far behind, hidden by the curve of the globe, and that was, perhaps, why his radio signals had not been received and answered by Woomera. The ultra-short waves, travelling only in straight lines, could not reach beyond the horizon.

Jim made a swift mental calculation. The rocket was evidently travelling north-east, and had covered roughly one-third of the distance round the earth in about forty minutes. It would be at least another hour before Australia came in sight again. There was nothing to do but wait, and hope that his tumultuous departure had brought someone to the site in time to save the control gear.

He stayed crouched by the viewing port, watching the marvellous panorama of the earth below. Soon he noticed a change. To the north of the globe a slowly-widening band of jet black sky had become visible, crowded with stars of fantastic brilliance, infinitely brighter than are ever seen on earth. Jim watched, fascinated, until he realized with a start of dismay, that the earth had vanished completely, and he was staring into the awful gulf of infinite space itself. A wave of vertigo swept over him, followed by panic terror. Were all his calculations wrong, and was the rocket still plunging out into the void?

He went quickly back to the instruments. The altimeter had not moved from its previous reading. As a blinding beam of sunlight shot through the port, and swung slowly across the cabin, the explanation came to him. The rocket was revolving slowly on its own axis, that was all. With a sigh of relief, he sank into his chair, only to start up a moment later, as a sudden devil's tattoo upon the outer skin of the rocket sounded from end to end of the ship. What on earth—or in space—was that?

The sharp rattling, particularly shocking after the absolute quiet of a moment before, lasted only a few minutes, and Jim soon guessed what it was. The rocket had passed through a meteor shower, and the tiny fragments of matter, little larger than grains of sand, but travelling at tremendous velocity, had bombarded the ship like machine-gun bullets. He knew it was extremely unlikely that he would encounter a meteorite of any size, but, if he did, it would probably rip through the toughened steel like a high-velocity shell. He shuddered, and looked again at the clock. Still half an hour to go.

*   *   *

In the control tower at Woomera, a state of intense but controlled excitement prevailed. Half an hour ago, Jim's first signals had been picked up by the radio telescope at Cape Canaveral, in Florida, and, although they had not been able to reply, the Americans had computed the rocket's probable orbit, and had passed the information on to England. Ten minutes later, Jodrell Bank was tracking the rocket by radar, since Jim had stopped transmitting, and the precise orbit had been calculated.

All the information had been sent on to Woomera, where the radio telescope on the tower had been accurately aligned to pick up Jim's signal as soon as the rocket came within range. Dr. Ballantyne, outwardly as icily calm as ever, but inwardly seething with excitement, sat at the remote control panel, ready to take over from his son at the first possible moment.

Jim was high above the Indian Ocean when he again switched on the transmitter. This side of the earth was still in darkness, so he was going by the clock. Almost at once his signal was answered, and a great wave of relief swept over the boy as he heard his father's voice: "Hello, son! No time for chit-chat, just listen. Switch on the radar scanner, turn the transmitter to full power, and plug in all the remote control units. You know the drill. Then hold tight. We'll bring you down, never fear. Fix your harness: the deceleration will be pretty fierce. Good luck, lad!"

With a grin at the terse instructions, Jim did as he was bid, and leaned back, knowing that he and his ship were now in the most competent hands on earth. The gyro-motors began to hum beneath his feet, and the rocket slowly swung until the main jets were pointing forwards. Then came a deep, shuddering vibration as the motors fired, almost soundless in the absence of the atmosphere, and the mounting pressure of deceleration forced him down into his seat. He blacked out.

When he came round, he was weightless again, for the rocket was now falling in a long parabola towards Australia. Again the motors roared briefly, to check the descent, and his weight came back. Jim thrilled to hear the mighty roar; he was within the atmosphere!

Despite repeated warnings about the danger, a considerable crowd had gathered outside the perimeter fence at Woomera, although the sun had not yet risen. A great cheer went up as the rocket came down from the zenith like a lift, balancing marvellously on its fiery tail, and made a perfect landing. Jim had been told to stay where he was until the launching platform cooled. When Dr. Ballantyne unlocked the entry port with his emergency key, and went into the control cabin, he found the boy curled up in the pilot's chair, fast asleep!

The Director touched his son's arm, and he woke at once.

"Hello, dad," he said. "Any damage?"

"Not a scratch, Jim."

"Good-oh! Then the moon trip's still on?"

"Certainly. Your little spin has saved us a lot of tests. Everything worked perfectly."

"Let me go with them, dad. *Please!*"

Dr. Ballantyne smiled: "Afraid they might damage your precious ship if you're not around? All right, son, I reckon you've earned it."

HOW TO EXAMINE WATERMARKS

by

L. N. and M. WILLIAMS

DIFFERENCES in watermarks can be very important on stamps and sometimes a variation, invisible from the front of the stamp, will make a rarity of an apparently common specimen. The most usual method of examining watermarks is to place the stamp face downwards on a shiny black surface, and examine the back of the specimen. Often the watermark will show up quite clearly and enable you to see whether it conforms to the normal type; but some watermarks are obstinate, and you will have to take further steps if you want them to show up well. As a rule, a few drops of benzine or lighter fuel, poured on the stamp while it lies in the black tray, will suffice—but this method is dangerous.

In the first place lighter fuel and benzine are highly inflammable, and you must take every precaution to assure that even the fumes do not come into contact with a naked light. Another drawback to the use of these volatile fluids is that they are quite unsuitable on stamps printed by photogravure, such as the current low values of Great Britain. If you put benzine on photogravure specimens the design will begin to dissolve and eventually becomes seriously damaged.

It is because of these disadvantages that philatelists have tried to discover another way of examining watermarks and, working on a well-known fact, a firm of dealers produced an instrument which, in many cases, solved the difficulty. The instrument, called the *Philatector*, consists of a series of colour filters, a slide to hold the stamp, a pocket lamp, and a battery. The stamp is placed in the slide, the light switched on, and the colour filters changed until one is found as near as possible to the colour in which the stamp is printed. Viewed through the correct filter, the stamp's design becomes practically invisible and the watermark shows up through what appears to be blank paper. It is a useful instrument, and one which many collectors have added to their philatelic kit.

If funds will not run to a *Philatector*, you can make a substitute which will help you to see quite a number of obstinate watermarks. Take a piece of stout white cardboard, measuring about eight inches by four inches, and cut six evenly spaced holes along each eight-inch side, each $\frac{3}{4}$ inch in diameter. Next buy twelve pieces of coloured celluloid or Cellophane, each in a different colour, and stick one of them over every hole on the back of the cardboard, so that the light shines through each hole in a different colour. The choice of colours is optional, but choose shades frequently used in stamp printing if possible.

Place the stamp you want to examine face upwards on the colour most closely approximating that of the design, and hold the specimen and the card against a bright light, so that the light shines right through the paper and celluloid. If you have chosen your colour correctly, and always provided that the stamp has a watermark, you will be able to see it against a background of colour.

COUNTRIES PUZZLE

THESE 64 squares contain the names of eight countries. One of them starts with the letters GU. Start with these two letters and by connecting other adjacent letters, left or right, up or down, or diagonally, find the eight names. (*Solution on page 192*)

D	I	Y	T	A	M	R	L
N	O	A	N	E	E	A	A
S	U	N	A	G	M	I	B
I	E	G	R	N	A	U	R
R	A	F	T	C	L	S	A
L	E	Z	E	I	E	G	P
E	A	T	N	G	W	A	I
N	I	N	D	A	R	S	N

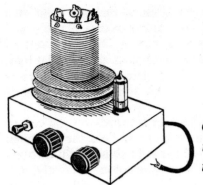

MAKE A ONE-VALVE RECEIVER

GILBERT DAVEY shows you how to make a simple tuning coil and incorporate it in a one-valve set.

THE TUNING COIL

EVERY receiver must have a coil which is tuned to the frequency of the station it is desired to receive, and the more complex the receiver the more coils it will have. The construction of this coil is described first and with it you can build a crystal receiver, or a transistor set for louder volume, and follow that with a one-valve set. Each of these receivers uses just the one coil. This progressive series will interest both beginners and keen experimenters.

The first thing to do is to make the coil; for this you will need a piece of cardboard or paxolin tubing 2 in. in diameter and about 4 in. long. Also you will need some odd pieces of card and half a dozen 6 B.A. bolts with a dozen nuts and washers. The wire used is 28 s.w.g. d.c.c. and you want a quarter-pound. The abbreviations mean, by the way, standard wire gauge and double-cotton-covered. First, let us consider the former on which we make our coil. If you can obtain one of bakelite or paxolin it would be ideal, but tubes of these materials are difficult to find these days. A piece of cardboard tubing such as is used for sending documents through the post, or for containing plans, can probably be purchased at a stationer's shop and its outer diameter should be 2 in. The medium-wave coil will be wound on with the turns side by side but the reaction and long-wave windings are "pile-wound" in slots which are made by means of three rings cut out of some stiff card. These rings have an internal diameter of 2 in. to match the external diameter of the tube on to which they must firmly fit. The external diameter of the rings is about $2\frac{1}{4}$ in. which will give you, when fitted to the tube, two slots, side by side, each $\frac{3}{4}$ in. deep. Figure 1 makes all this clear.

If you want to make your coil former really effective it can be given a coat of shellac varnish both inside and out and then baked dry and hard in an oven. The rings should be treated similarly. This will prevent dampness in the air or changes of temperature being able to affect the somewhat absorbent cardboard former and causing a deterioration in the coil's efficiency. If you live in a humid climate, and I know many readers live outside the British Isles, it is essential to give the former the shellac varnish treatment before winding the coil and then to shellac varnish the whole of the coil again after it is wound so that the cotton covering of the coils cannot be affected by the damp. The treated coils must be dried gently (not baked) in a warm oven or hot sunshine.

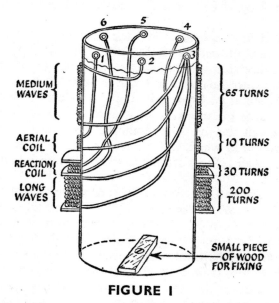

FIGURE I

Having obtained your coil former and cut out the rings, varnished them if you intend doing so, the next step is to fit the six nuts and bolts to the top of the former at equal distances round it about ⅛ in. from the top edge. The round head of the bolt with a washer should be inside the tube and another washer and a nut on the outside. The extra nut is for external wiring purposes. Do not tighten the nuts and bolts at this stage; "finger-tight" will be adequate as the various wires of the coil have to be connected to them. Next with pencil, or, preferably, ball-point pen, mark the former beside each nut with its number, starting at 1 and ending beside it at 6. Figure 1 makes all these points clear and you must, of course, take care that the nuts and bolts are well spaced so that there is no possibility of one touching another; the circumference of a 2-in. diameter former is over 6 in. so that there is room for an inch spacing between the bolts.

Use a Cocoa Tin

Note that you cannot use any form of metal tubing for coil-winding although there is no objection to constructing a cardboard tube by winding it around a tin, such as a cocoa tin, of the right diameter and sticking it down along the edges. But do use stout cardboard if you use this method, as otherwise the tube will collapse when the wire is wound on it.

The former being completed and the terminals in place at the top edge you can now proceed to wind on the wire. All the windings must be in the same direction so that I suggest you take the former with the top, i.e. the end with the nuts and bolts, in your left hand and wind on the wire with your right hand, winding always away from your body so that all the time the direction of winding will always be the same. If you have to put the job down unfinished you can remember quite easily the direction in which the windings went so as to maintain this when you start again. If you are left handed, of course, you will reverse the hands.

In a well-made coil all connections are taken through the former and up inside the coil to the terminals (those are the nuts and bolts you have fixed at the top). To start winding make two holes in the former about a $\frac{1}{4}$ in. from the top just below terminal No. 2, tiny holes such as a darning-needle would make, and thread the end of your wire through one hole into the former and up out of the former through the second hole and down through the first hole again. You will find the end of the wire now is inside the former and is anchored firmly to it.

Bare that end of wire and loop it neatly round under the washer of terminal No. 2 (you will have to loosen it a little to do this). Having made a neat connection here tighten up terminal 2 carefully with spanner or pliers. Now carefully wind on your coil-former sixty-five turns of wire, each turn closely and neatly touching the previous one. It is a good idea to push the turns together with your thumb-nail from time to time as you wind but do not let any of the turns overlap. When you have completed sixty-five turns cut the wire, leaving 4 in. or so for connecting, make two small holes and, as before, in, out, in and fix the wire firmly to the former, making sure it is pulled tight so that all the turns of the coil are kept compactly together.

The end of the wire now inside the tube should be bared and connected to terminal No. 3 but do not fix the terminal firmly yet as other wires must go on it. Next wind on ten turns for the aerial winding commencing about the space of one turn away from the last winding and fixing the coil by means of two small holes in the former at the beginning and end as before. The commencing wire of this ten-turn coil should be connected to terminal No. 1 (tighten up after connection) and the end of it goes to terminal No. 3 (do not tighten yet). Having finished the ten-turn aerial coil the first ring must be fixed to the former and the position for this is $\frac{1}{4}$ in. away from the bottom of the last winding.

Slide it on the former and force a little adhesive (preferably the waterproof type) between it and the coil former so as to glue them together. The next ring can then be fixed in the same way $\frac{1}{4}$ in. apart from the first, and then the third one leaving a space of $\frac{1}{2}$ in. from the second one. You will now have to leave the former to dry overnight so that the rings are well fixed as the wire will strain them somewhat.

In the first ($\frac{1}{4}$ in.) slot, the reaction winding of thirty turns is wound. Fix the wire at the beginning, as before, but simply wind the wire in the slot higgledy-piggledy, thirty turns of it. At the end you will have no room to make two holes, you will have to push your needle down the slot to make one hole and thread the end of your wire through it. If you pull it tight it should hold quite well. The beginning of this winding goes to terminal No. 5 and the end to No. 6, both terminals being tightened up.

Finally, the long-wave winding consists of 200 turns wound "anyhow" in the last slot to fill it completely. Start off by fixing your wire with two little holes, joining its bared end to terminal No. 3 with the other two wires on it; the terminal can then be tightened up. You can finish off by making a needle hole through the edge of the last ring threading the wire through it and through another hole at the foot of the former up to terminal No. 4 to which its bared end can be connected and the nut tightened up. That completes connections to all the terminals and the coil is made.

It is fixed to a baseboard or chassis by making a small fillet of wood, with a central screw-hole, just to fit inside the coil-former at the foot with the aid of a spot of glue. A screw or nut and bolt through the hole will fix the coil firmly. The connections to the coil are shown in Figure 2. An on-off switch across terminals 3 and 4 is required for long-wave purposes. When open it gives long-waves, and when shut medium-waves.

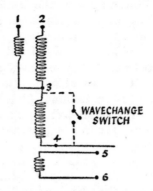

FIGURE 2   COIL CONNECTIONS

MAKING THE ONE-VALVE RECEIVER

Components List

Coil—home-made

C.1 Variable condenser, solid dielectric 500 pF.

C.2 Fixed condenser 100 pF ceramic or mica.

C.3 Fixed condenser ·1 mF electrolytic or paper 150-volt wkg.

C.4 Variable condenser, solid dielectric or air dielectric 100 pF.

R.1 Resistor 2·2 MΩ $\frac{1}{2}$-watt⎫
    (or smaller will do)   ⎬ 20 per cent.
R.2 Resistor 10 KΩ $\frac{1}{2}$-watt ⎪tolerance
R.3 Resistor 22 KΩ $\frac{1}{2}$-watt ⎭

On-off switch, B7G valveholder, Two 2-hole socket strips.

Wire, solder, 2 knobs to suit condenser spindles, wood or metal chassis. 6 B.A. nuts and bolts or wood screws.

Valve, 1T4 or Mullard DF91, etc. (see text).

Batteries 1·5 volt, 45 volt.

So far we have considered using the coil in two receivers, a crystal set and a two-transistor receiver. Both of these are limited in range because they can only pass into the headphones those signals received by the aerial which, after rectification by the germanium diode detector, are strong enough to be heard.

It is true that the transistors provide some amplification but this follows the diode and can only make louder what it has already received and rectified. These days we can obtain R.F. transistors which are used for amplifying the signals before they are *detected* by the diode and which allow greater range to be obtained. It is now possible to make all-transistor superhet receivers.

Before transistors were invented we always had to use valves and had a screen-grid or pentode valve in the radio-frequency stage to give range, a similar type in the detector stage with a pentode or power-valve in the output stage. This is known as a T.R.F. set. The detector stage generally had a device called *reaction* incorporated in it and this, by feeding back some of the energy at the anode of the valve into its grid, enables minute signals to be greatly amplified. Unless an R.F. stage is used, careless use of reaction can cause the feedback to affect the aerial circuit and allow interference with other receivers in the neighbourhood, but this will not occur if you take care in using such a receiver. A superhet receiver, such as is normally used commercially today does not use reaction. Now study the one-valve receiver in Figure 3.

This one-valve receiver is simply the detector section of a T.R.F. receiver. There is thus no R.F. stage for range and no audio frequency stage to make the signals louder after detection, but it has reaction and being a valve detector has the advantage of the amplification inherent in the valve itself. The disadvantages are the fragility of the valve compared with a transistor and, in addition to the low-voltage battery used

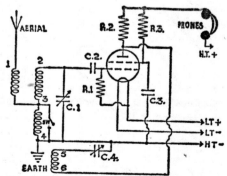

FIGURE 3   ONE-VALVE SCHEMATIC DIAGRAM

for filament heating, the need for a high-tension battery of between 45 and 90 volts.

The type of valve used is a miniature radio-frequency pentode which takes a filament voltage of 1·4, and which is quite easily supplied from a 1·5-volt dry battery. Four types of valve are suitable, namely, the 1T4 which is an International type made by a number of makers and of which, in the Mullard range, the equivalent is the DF 91. Both take a filament current of 50 milliamps, as does the Mullard DF 92 which is also suitable. The DF 96, also made by Mullard, could be used and is less expensive in current, taking only 25 milliamps. All these valves are interchangeable in the valveholder, which is a B7G type and for which the connections are shown in Figure 4.

The receiver is built on a small chassis 4 in. long by 6 in. wide by

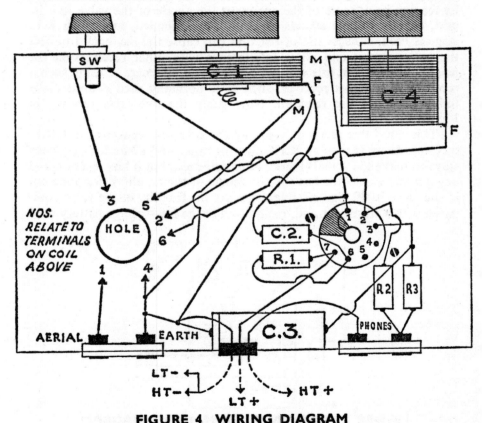

FIGURE 4   WIRING DIAGRAM

2 in. deep. I use a small metal one of aluminium but you can easily make up one of wood or plywood or wood and hardboard. What is required is a small box of which the two end-pieces are 4 in. by 2 in. by perhaps ½ in. thick. The other two sides are of hardboard 6 in. long by 2 in. and another piece of hardboard 6 in. by 4 in. makes the bottom of the box, or, when it is inverted, the top of the chassis. The whole thing is tacked together with ½-in. panel pins, a smear of glue having first been applied for strengthening purposes.

Along the front are fixed the wavechange switch, in the centre is the tuning condenser, and then comes the reaction condenser. The chassis and positions for these are shown in Figure 5. On top of the chassis are fixed the coil and the valveholder. The coil is fixed by wedging and gluing a small fillet of wood beneath it and then bolting or screwing that to the chassis. Somewhere alongside that piece of wood and underneath the coil you must drill out a hole about ½-in. in diameter through which the wires can pass through the chassis and up inside the coil to the terminals at its top. A ½-in. diameter hole is also needed for the B7G valveholder.

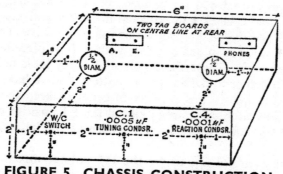

FIGURE 5   CHASSIS CONSTRUCTION

Wiring-up the Receiver

Wiring-up the receiver is quite a simple task with a lightweight instrument soldering-iron and resin-cored solder. The point to bear in mind is the need for absolute cleanliness in order to solder successfully. The bit of the iron must be clean and so must the work to be soldered. Rubbing the bit on a piece of old sandpaper should keep it clean and cleaning soldering tags with a corner of fine sand- or emery-paper should provide a good surface on which the solder will run.

If insulated tinned copper wire is used for connecting purposes the removal of a fraction of an inch of sleeving at the end should leave exposed a piece of wire clean enough for soldering. The reason for the small holes in the tags fitted to components is to allow the wire or wires to be pushed through and bent round and so held fast. The *hot* iron and solder are both applied together, the solder runs and a good joint is made (provided all was clean to start with).

Note that the tuning condensers have moving and fixed plates, designated on diagrams respectively as *M* or *F* and connections must be correctly made as marked. The moving plates will automatically be earthed to chassis by their fixing collars and nuts if a metal chassis is used, but it is as well to make the direct connection to the plates as well. The electrolytic condenser is *polarized* and has to be connected the correct way round with its positive side to the valveholder pin and the other, or negative pole, to earth. There are various methods of marking these condensers, either with $+$ or a red sign for positive and $-$ or black for negative at the appropriate ends, or, possibly, merely a black ring around the end which is to be connected to the negative and earth side of the circuit.

Three wires are needed for connecting to the batteries, and in the original set I used a black PVC-covered flex for negative, a similar one in red for HT positive and a yellow one for LT positive. The two negatives, HT and LT, are joined together with a short piece of wire at the batteries themselves. These three coloured wires look neatest if they are braided together and tied at the battery end. I have not used a battery on-off switch in this receiver in order to keep the cost as low as possible. To switch off simply pull out the LT positive plug. Do not forget to do this after using the set otherwise the batteries will soon run down.

Do be very careful not to get the HT voltage mixed up with the LT side as the valve will soon "blow". It is a good idea to test the LT circuit before inserting the valve by connecting up all batteries and 'phones, then, by pushing two pieces of bare wire down the sockets numbered 1 and 7 (each side of the blank space) see if a flash-lamp bulb lights when touched across them. If it does, all is well, if it flashes up and burns out the HT is obviously in the wrong place and must be rectified before the valve is used. For economy always buy the largest battery you can afford. A final word, be careful of oscillating, it causes interference. The right-hand knob works the reaction, use it to bring up the volume to the point just below that where the valve oscillates.

TEN-MINUTE MYSTERY

by

LEONARD GRIBBLE

WHEN Superintendent Slade was called to investigate a robbery at Lightam Grange he found that Colonel and Mrs. Rudge, the owners, had been away at the time. Stevens, their gardener, told the Yard man he left work at half-past five that afternoon and cycled home. He was standing in a summer-house at shortly after four o'clock, taking shelter from a brief but heavy shower, when he saw a cyclist in shorts and vest pedalling up the lane leading towards the Grange drive.

"Matter of fact, I was mending a puncture while I waited," he admitted.

A few minutes later, just after the rain had stopped, he noticed the cyclist pedalling back down the lane. Slade found evidence that the study window had been forced. The housekeeper had gone to visit her sick sister.

Slade discovered tracks of two worn cycle tyres in muddy ooze in the lane mentioned by Stevens. The tracks ran mostly to the left of the lane going towards the main road. Next the Yard man visited the "Copper Kettle," a popular café on the main road not far away.

"We had a cycling club here that afternoon," Bert Jones, the proprietor, told Slade. "They arrived about ten to four and by the time they left the storm had passed, so they didn't put on their macs."

"Did any of them leave during the storm?" Slade asked.

"They might have done," said Jones. "I can't say. But they certainly all paid for their teas."

Questioned again, Stevens admitted that he didn't get a good look at the cyclist's face and couldn't remember the colour of his hair. Colonel Rudge said only money had been taken, from a desk in the study. Slade found that the cycle tracks did not correspond with the new tyres on Stevens' cycle. However, the Yard man went to Colonel Rudge and said, "I'm arresting your gardener, Colonel."

What was Slade's theory which justified arrest? All the necessary clues are given. Solution on page 192.

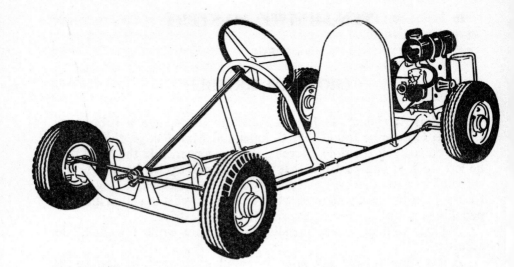

THE SPORT OF GO-KARTING

by

CHARLES FOTHERGILL

IF you are reading your *Boy's Own Companion* sometime during the weekend, then you can be sure that some lucky "teenager" not far away is helping his parents to load up "the family racer". "The racer" in this case is not some high-powered and complicated Grand Prix formula model of the type in which you might see Stirling Moss chasing Jack Brabham at Silverstone or Rheims, but a kart. Do not be misled by that simple title. The kart is so light and small that in some cases it can be packed into the luggage boot of the family saloon; it is more often carried on the roof. Yet it is a pukka racing machine.

The kart, which in effect is really only a steel platform with wheels at the four corners and an engine to push, can be bought in kit form to be assembled at home for as little as £25. You can pay six times as much for an engine alone but the kart remains basically the same with this wide variation of prices and performances. That is why, with its simplicity of control and safety, the kart provides fun for the whole family. Prince Charles is a kart enthusiast and has a model of his own.

In 1959 I went to the Isle of Wight to try out one of the first British karts. This model was powered by a 79·7 c.c. Jap engine with a primary chain, jockey and belt drive operating on the nearside wheel. There was a right foot pedal for the throttle and the left foot pedal controlled the combined clutch and brake. We had great fun driving this little machine on a slab of concrete left by wartime defenders and the maximum speed of 35 m.p.h. which was attained seemed tremendous because of our close proximity to the ground.

Since 1959 there has been very great progress in karting. Instead of just pottering about in what might be described as home-made and rather badly-designed karts with hack lawn-mower type engines, we now have karts that come from the drawing board to the workshop in the most advanced manner. The engines used now are no longer the low horse-power lawn-mower type but race-bred two-stroke motors that have been adapted and modified by the manufacturers especially for kart racing, and we have exciting examples offered us by Germany, Italy, America, France, and Britain.

The sport is still open to everyone but it is faster and safer than it was in 1959—safer because after much experience the kart manufacturers are now building machines that have a really astonishing power to weight ratio; they are properly constructed and well balanced, have excellent brakes and steering, and will handle well under all conditions. Speeds of up to 70 m.p.h. can now be obtained on the straight.

The Royal Automobile Club, as the governing body of motor sport in this country, has now taken a hand in the control of kart racing and lays down some very strict rules. For example, karts taking part in any officially recognized races now must meet the following requirements: the wheel-base not to exceed 50 inches, with a minimum of 40 inches, and the maximum overall length of the vehicle not to exceed 72 inches. There is also a maximum height of 24 inches measured from the ground. Usually the kart's ground clearance is between two and three inches.

In 1961 the R.A.C. ran a British Kart Championship at Brands Hatch, where about 80 drivers took part, and the champion proved to be Anthony Sisson, of Hucknall, Nottinghamshire, driving a *Progress* kart. The course used was 740 yards of the famous Brands Hatch circuit and this lap, which had to be covered 20 times, embraced six corners and a straight on which some of these little machines were claimed to reach 70 m.p.h. The lady winner was Ann Thorp, a 23-year-old secretary from Alderminster, Stratford-upon-Avon.

A class winner was Johnny Brise, of Wilmington, Dartford, Kent.

one of our greatest kart aces, who builds and sells his own machines. Needless to say, his son Johnny, aged 9, is also an expert performer although not yet old enough to take part in races.

There are about 100 clubs in Britain now and 27 members of the British Kart Manufacturers' Association. Most of the latter are small engineering companies but we do have people like John Buckler, of Reading, well known for his 1,172 c.c. racing cars, employing a modified Ford engine, Jim Russell, of Norfolk, and other experienced "racing types" building these special karts. We now have 50 officially-approved kart racing circuits, but there is still a long way to go. America has over 100,000, and France over 200!

International Karting

Karting now has an international flavour, with events held in all parts of Europe, and this year the international governing body of motor sport has laid down that only class 1 and 2—that is for 100 c.c. machines and 200 c.c. machines, both without gearbox, should be eligible. There are other elements brought into these classes by the clubs. One thing is a price limit, which prevents the wealthy enthusiast picking up all the awards. For instance, there are sub-sections which enable races to be run for karts with engines costing not more than £25. Then there is a limit of £40 and soon up to "the sky's the limit" sort of thing. Class 4, which has been discarded by the international authority, seems to be for British karts only. This makes eligible motor-cycle engines of 200 c.c. with a gearbox. One can appreciate the necessity for this price limit when I mention that you can now buy engines costing £100 (the Bultaco) and in Class 2 power units costing £150, such as the twin Parillas.

In 1961 a particularly interesting event was the Six Heures Internationale de Paris, where there were 48 entries from ten European countries. This was raced over a 1,000 yards circuit with many twists but a really fast straight so that the average winning speeds were just short of 40 m.p.h. There was £800 offered in prizes. For youngsters a great chance came when the firm responsible for the Lambretta scooter sales in this country advertised a Trokart kit for £25, and needless to say the firm was simply swamped with orders. It is much cheaper to buy a kart in kit form and assemble it at home because there is no purchase tax to pay. While £25 must be the minimum cost of a kart, prices reach £200 for the faster machines needed for competitions.

PLATE 4. Karting is an exciting sport. The two boys seen above are testing Trokarts at Croydon. Douglas Meekins, 17 (Welwyn Wheelers, Herts.) much prefers two wheels (left). In 1961 he took fifth place in the National 12-hour Cycle Championship and broke the junior record with a mileage of 258.747 (average over 21 m.p.h.)

PLATE 5. A set of masks made from papier mâché. A successful mask exaggerates any outstanding features.

FUN WITH MASKS

by

DEREK HILLESLEY

MAKING masks can give a great deal of pleasure and satisfaction. A great deal of artistic ability is not required to produce a good mask. The secret of successful mask-making lies in the over-exaggeration of the salient features of the character being produced. The latter include those lines and characteristics that give the impression of age, mood, or racial type. A double chin must really bulge; negroid lips must be very full; and frightened eyes must stand out as much as the drooping corners of a sour mouth. The beginner should not undertake to carve a mask out of a chunk of wood. Early attempts should be made out of papier mâché, which fortunately is light, strong, and easy to handle.

The first thing you require is clay. This may be taken from your garden or some nearby claypit or excavation, or bought from a craft shop. Prepare enough of this to model the required size of the face in relief. This is best done on a piece of board, and all you must remember is to concentrate on the features you wish to exaggerate. In fact everything must be exaggerated to a greater or lesser extent. Once the shape has dried, further work can start by mixing some paper-hangers' paste with water, until it is fairly thick. Strips of newspaper are then torn into pieces about one inch wide, and in turn they are dipped in the paste, and laid over the clay face. Once one layer has been put on, another can follow, making sure that everything is covered by crossing the strips and pressing them down on the model. Even layers on the entire surface are ensured if a coloured newspaper is used alternately with the white. This continues until some thirty layers have been added, and then it is left to dry.

Some days later the dry papier mâché shell can be lifted off the original shape, and once the edges have been trimmed with scissors, the rough sections can be gently smoothed with fine sandpaper. If to be worn, the eyes can be cut out, and then the job can be painted. A coat of size will prime the mask if enamel is to be used, but otherwise tempera colours can be applied directly. Further character can be introduced by the use of raffia, wool, or theatrical hair. Brush bristle eyebrows and a drooping string moustache also serve well.

HOW DO BIRDS NAVIGATE?

by

R. S. R. FITTER

THE bristle-thighed curlew, which nests only on the coast of Alaska, winters six thousand miles away on a number of islands in mid-Pacific, including Hawaii and Tahiti. Another North American bird, the jack-pine or Kirtland's warbler, breeds only in a restricted area in the state of Michigan and winters only in the Bahamas off the coast of Florida.

The survival of both these species thus depends on the birds possessing an accurate sense of navigation, for a bird which makes a sea crossing to a small island must reach its destination or perish in the ocean. The bristle-thighed curlew makes an uninterrupted sea passage of at least two thousand miles. Kirtland's warbler has a much shorter sea passage, but if it over-shoots the mark it flies off into the open Atlantic. Clearly the bird's internal directional mechanism must be particularly accurate in these cases, but there is reason to suppose that it is nearly as accurate in most, if not all, species of migratory birds.

Our own British swallow, for instance, returns often to the same barn or outhouse in England year after year to breed, having made a round trip to South Africa in the meantime. Moreover, it is possible that they make the trip to Africa to the same district each year. There is increasing evidence that birds become as attached to specific wintering grounds as they do to specific breeding grounds. Peter Scott's white-fronted geese at the Wildfowl Trust grounds at Slimbridge, in Gloucestershire, are a case in point. They come every year, as they have done for many years past, to the same grassy flats.

So it is very probable that the pattern of Kirtland's warbler is repeated in every migratory bird. Its whole life is spent in shuttling backwards and forwards between two cabbage patches, which may be thousands of miles apart. In the case of our resident birds, such as the corn bunting, the territories may be only a few miles apart. A bird must be able to navigate somehow even to get to the other side of an English county. We see this power of navigation put to practical use in the homing pigeon. Rock-doves, from which our domestic pigeons are descended, are not migratory, yet pigeons do have a strong sense of their home loft. Pigeon-fanciers spend an immense amount of time and trouble in training their birds, but recent experiments have suggested that even untrained pigeons may have a good sense of the direction in which their home loft lies.

Pigeons have presumably been chosen as homers because they are easy to keep and rear in captivity, for many other birds can also be used as homers. Even Noah used a raven as well as a dove, and in a Sumerian version of the Flood legend, swallows were used as well. Pliny tells us of a Roman racehorse owner who used painted swallows as messengers to report the result of races, relying on the fact that they would be sure to return to their own nests! At one time, too, the natives of some Pacific islands used frigate-birds for sending messages to each other.

In recent years many ornithologists have carried out experiments with the homing power of wild birds, and have obtained some astonishing results, especially during the breeding season. Outside the breeding season the farthest a bird has returned is 434 miles; this was a black-headed gull. The record distance during the breeding season is held by another sea-bird, the Manx shearwater. One of these birds was taken from its nest on the island of Skokholm, off the coast of Pembrokeshire, and transported across the Atlantic to Boston, Massachusetts. Twelve and a half days after it was released at Boston, 3,050 miles from its home, it was found again in its own burrow on Skokholm. It actually beat the postal authorities by half a day, for the news that it had been released at Boston arrived by post ten hours after the bird itself had arrived! Another history-making Manx shearwater was sent from

115

Skokholm to Venice by air on July 7, 1937, by R. M. Lockley. Venice, at the head of the Adriatic Sea, is 2,700 miles from Skokholm by sea, and 930 miles by the direct overland route. This bird returned to its burrow on July 23, having taken some 14 days 5 hours on its journey from the Venice Lido.

All this is very baffling. Among other birds that have returned home over distances of more than five hundred miles during the breeding season are the white stork, herring gull, alpine swift, swallow, wryneck, red-backed shrike, and starling. Even the stay-at-home house sparrow has returned from six miles away. How is it all done? We are faced with one of the great surviving mysteries of biology, but it is a mystery that is slowly yielding its secrets to painstaking scientific research. One thing is already clear. There is no magic about it, nothing that will take us outside the known realms of science.

Birds Navigate by the Sun

It is clear that birds navigate, like anybody else, by the sun, though it is still not clear as to what mechanism they use. People often try to solve mysteries by invoking all kinds of ingenious solutions, only to be driven back eventually to commonsense, which is where they ought to have started. Many theories have been propounded to account for a bird's evident ability to navigate. One of the simplest is that birds recognize the route by visible landmarks. This seems to be the basis of the training of race pigeons, which are taken progressively greater distances from their home loft, so that they will be able to learn the route home. No doubt this is an element in the location of the final destination, but we already know that completely untrained pigeons are quite capable of orienting themselves in the right direction when released in a strange country.

Another group of theories has tried to prove that the magnetism of the earth and the Coriolis force have something to do with it. Birds have even been released with magnets tied to their wings to counter the effects of the earth's magnetism. Most elaborate experiments have taken place in the United States to try and prove the Coriolis force theory, but all to no avail. It has been suggested that birds may detect familiar smells in the atmosphere, and that this could be counteracted by hanging stale fish in the travelling box!

Another fantastic theory was that a bird could remember all the turns and twists taken in its outward journey while it was in a darkened box. Birds have been transported while under an anaesthetic, but this has made no difference to their homing ability in the later experiments. As long ago as 1906 it was first suggested that birds might navigate by the sun, but as so often happens, the correct solution was almost completely ignored. However, recent experiments in Germany have left little doubt that it is the sun which enables migratory birds to find their way in the right direction. This does not explain how they know what *is* the right direction, but when they could not see the sun birds scattered in all directions. When the sun was out they all went west or north-west. This experiment was carried out with caged starlings at a time when they would normally be migrating west or north-west. Even more striking were the experiments with mirrors that appeared to change the position of the sun; then the starlings navigated according to the sun's apparent position.

The work of von Frisch who demonstrated in Austria the ability of bees to navigate by means of polarized light, which need not come directly from the sun, naturally aroused hopes that this might also be proved for birds. But the German starling experiments showed that when the birds could only see the polarized light coming from a blue sky they were just as puzzled as when the sky was overcast. So it is the sun or nothing, and birds that migrate at night must fly on the bearing obtained by them before the sun set. If the wind changes during the night and carries them off course, so much the worse for the birds!

G. V. T. Matthews, a leading British authority on this subject, believes that recent experiments have determined without doubt that birds must have some internal chronometer mechanism that enables them to navigate by instinctively calculating changes in the sun-arc, even when they have only had a sight of the sun some hours before.

INDOOR FLYING MODELS

*Turn your clubroom into an indoor flying field with
these attractive models—simple, sturdy and inexpensive*

by R. H. WARRING

MAKE your own clubroom a flying field with R.T.P. (round-the-pole) models. Flights of two minutes or more are possible within the confines of even an average-size room at home—if you think that is a short flight, just watch the second hand of a watch making two revolutions! There is very little chance of damage to furniture *or* models because they are flown on a cotton line in circles. Just adjust the line length to clear all obstacles, wind the motor—and away you go. Details of a simple, sturdy model for R.T.P. flying are given in the cut-away drawing. Wing span is 16 in., so the first step is to get a piece of drawing paper at least this length and on it mark out the fuselage, wing, tailplane, and fin shapes, working from the dimensioned plan given. All the shapes are simple and designed for easy drawing up, and building.

Balsa Noseblock

Actual size patterns are given for the ribs, propeller blade (two required), cabin parts, formers, and noseblock unit. Trace or transfer these with carbon paper carefully on to sheet balsa (of the thickness noted) and cut out accurately. Fuselage side frames are built flat over the full-size drawing in the usual manner. Assemble on the two formers and then cement in the cross spacers. Then cover with tissue, water-spray and finally give one coat of clear dope when dry. Cabin parts are cemented in place to complete, covering in the front of the cabin with a thin piece of celluloid. The wing has no dihedral and is built as a flat panel, covered with tissue on the top surface only. Tailplane and fin are simple frames, again covered on one side only. Do *not* water-spray *or* dope these parts. All are cemented in place on the fuselage.

Thinning Propellers

The noseblock and plug are cemented together and fitted with small tin bearings each side, pierced for the propeller shaft. Propeller blades are thinned down by sanding, and also shaped to an aerofoil section.

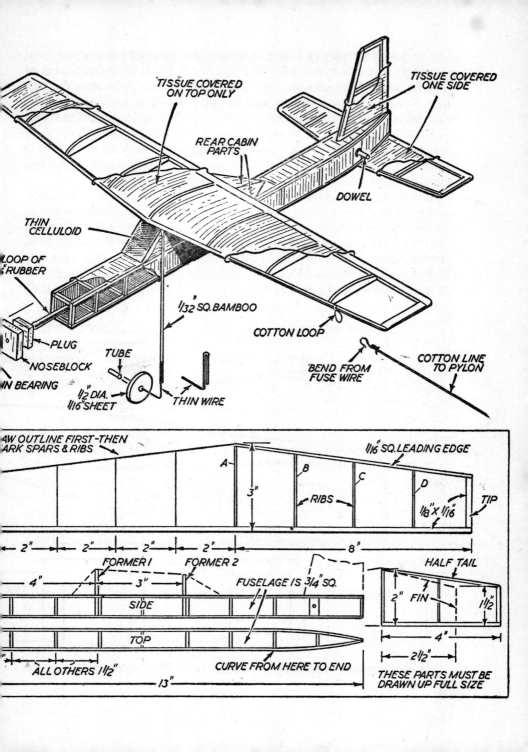

TISSUE COVERED ON TOP ONLY

REAR CABIN PARTS

TISSUE COVERED ONE SIDE

DOWEL

THIN CELLULOID

LOOP OF RUBBER

1/32" SQ. BAMBOO

COTTON LOOP

COTTON LINE TO PYLON

PLUG

TUBE

NOSEBLOCK

BEND FROM FUSE WIRE

N BEARING

1/2" DIA. 1/16" SHEET

THIN WIRE

DRAW OUTLINE FIRST—THEN MARK SPARS & RIBS

1/16" SQ. LEADING EDGE

A   B   C   D

3"

RIBS

TIP

1/8" X 1/16"

2"   2"   2"   2"   8"

FORMER 1   FORMER 2

HALF TAIL

4"   3"

FUSELAGE IS 3/4" SQ.

2"   FIN   1 1/2"

SIDE

TOP

4'

CURVE FROM HERE TO END

2 1/2"

ALL OTHERS 1 1/2"

THESE PARTS MUST BE DRAWN UP FULL SIZE

13"

The hubs are circular in shape and plug into a small tube rolled from gumstrip. Wind this tube around a piece of 3/16-in. diameter dowel or anything else of similar size. The blades should be a tight fit in the hub tube so that they can be twisted to a pitch angle and adjusted, as necessary, for best results. A cotton loop on the wing leading edge forms an attachment point for the cotton line. The pylon or "pole" can be of dowel or any similar hard wood, mounted in a heavy base. A simple swivel is fitted to the top of the pole to take the other end of the line and it is important that this should turn quite freely.

If you want an undercarriage for making rise-off-ground flights, trim a leg to about 1/32-in. square from a bamboo split and cement to the side of the fuselage. Bind a thin wire axle to the lower end and fit a balsa wheel, using a smalled rolled gumstrip tube for the wheel hub. The propeller shaft is bent from 20 s.w.g. wire, passed through the two tin bearings in the noseblock unit and then turned over and bound to the propeller hub. If you bend a loop on the front end you can then

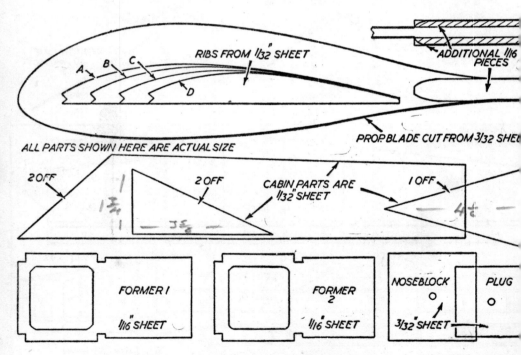

In this diagram, readers should take the noseblock as being ¾-in. square

use a winder to wind up the motor, which is so much easier than winding by hand.

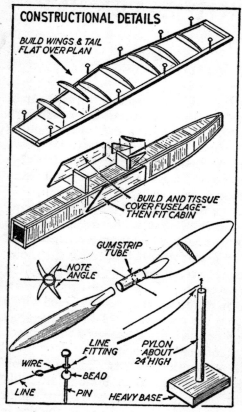

CONSTRUCTIONAL DETAILS

BUILD WINGS & TAIL FLAT OVER PLAN

BUILD AND TISSUE COVER FUSELAGE— THEN FIT CABIN

GUM STRIP TUBE

NOTE ANGLE

LINE FITTING

PYLON ABOUT 24" HIGH

WIRE

BEAD

LINE

PIN

HEAVY BASE

Trimming Troubles

The model should need little or no trimming. If it dives, warp up the rear (trailing edge) of the tailplane slightly; or add a little weight to the rear end of the fuselage. If it climbs too much, pack the top of nose-block down slightly (e.g. with a piece of 1/32-in. sheet cemented in position). All wood parts for the model—except the undercarriage leg and dowel for the rear rubber anchorage— are of balsa, of course. The lighter you can make the model the longer it will fly. The British record for this type of model, incidentally, is in the region of six minutes!

For best results the rubber motor must be lubricated, which should be done by smearing on rubber lubricant or castor oil— *not* ordinary lubricating oil. A 15-in. loop of 3/16-in. rubber will take about 1,000 turns maximum when properly lubricated and broken in, which means winding it up in stages at first. That is, never put on more than 500 turns on a new motor and gradually work up to maximum turns from that.

FENCING IS NOT EXPENSIVE

by

JOHN LEIGH

THE early morning walk and the silent, decisive meeting under the trees at dawn is, fortunately, a thing of the past. We have relinquished the sword in favour of the less romantic court of law and, as a means of settling personal disputes, the latter is more satisfactory. However, although duelling is now, for the most part, extinct, the sport of fencing is still very much alive. Fencing is one of the oldest of all sports. It seems probable that the Germanic races were responsible for its growth.

The use of gunpowder in warfare revolutionized the course of fencing, for when gunpowder came into fashion armour went out and the heavy, double-edged, battle sword was replaced by the more elegant, but equally deadly, rapier. It was soon discovered that although the rapier was useful in war it was cumbersome to carry about in time of peace and the much shorter court sword was developed. About this time the art of fencing came into its own. At first, the court sword was used with a dagger or with a cloak (to envelop the opponent's blade) but fencers soon realized that the sword could be used for defence as well as attack and this discovery marks the birth of modern fencing.

During the sixteenth and seventeenth centuries fencing schools became popular and no gentleman was equipped for life until he could handle a sword with skill. Since those days much has happened to fencing, far too much to be related here. Today, it is a sport which is increasing rapidly in popularity and thousands enjoy pleasure, excitement, and relaxation at some four hundred clubs in Britain. Three weapons are used in modern fencing; the foil, the epée, and the sabre. The foil is the basic weapon but the weapons vary considerably, both in form and in the technique involved. The foil is a light sword (the maximum weight must not exceed $17\frac{5}{8}$ ozs.) with a rectangular or square-section blade less than $43\frac{1}{4}$ inches in length. For foil the target is the trunk of the body from the seams of the fencing jacket on the shoulder down to, and including, the groin. Contests are generally fought for the best of nine hits, that is to say the first fencer to score five hits on his opponent is the winner.

According to the rules a fencer may gain a hit in any manner he chooses so long as the weapon is not thrown. In practice, however, unorthodoxy does not pay and fencers usually restrict themselves to various combinations of four or five well-tried basic attacks. The epée, which is a much heavier weapon, is really the old duelling sword. The few sword duels which have been fought in recent years have all been fought with this weapon. The epée should be used in the gymnasium as if a duel were being fought, for it is "the weapon of discretion".

As duels were normally fenced to first blood the whole of the body (trunk, limbs, and head) remains the target for epée. However, as every attack involves extending, and exposing, the sword-arm, the most common hit is probably that scored on the wrist or forearm of the unwary attacker. For competition purposes the first fencer to score three hits wins and modern electrical apparatus has made it possible to judge hits to within a 25th of a second. This last is essential in competition fencing as it is often impossible for the human eye to discern which of two hits was the first to land home and only the first counts. The sabre, as the name implies, is the academy version of the cavalry man's weapon. It differs from foil and epée in that hits can be scored with the whole of the front edge and a third of the back edge of the blade as well as with the point. In short, it is the weapon of cut and thrust. The target is everything above the waist and, like foil, competitions are for the best of nine hits.

Sabre fencing is usually very fast indeed and a few bouts can provide as much violent exercise as any normal person is likely to want in one evening. The hits, which must, if they are to be successful, be delivered at lightning speed, are executed with the fingers and wrist and should land lightly. The man who attempts to cut his opponent to ribbons by virtue of his brute strength is never a successful fencer.

Contrary to popular opinion fencing is not an expensive sport. The most expensive item of equipment is the canvas jacket which costs about £5. An all-purpose mask costs £1 10s. and a foil about £1. The other two weapons cost slightly more. Breeches can be improvised from a pair of cricket flannels and a soft leather glove gives the sword hand sufficient protection for foil fencing, although a specially padded canvas glove is needed when epée and sabre are being used. Many clubs own equipment which can be loaned to beginners while they save up to buy their own. Weapons, however, are personal things. Many clubs allow special rates for beginners and under-twenties.

HUNTERS OF TODAY

The forest burns with the sunset fire,
And we've six rough miles to tramp;
But we'll talk of a good day's hunting
As we're slogging it back to camp.

I caught that big lynx just as he turned,
Fierce-eyed, and crouched to the ground.
You bagged the bull moose down by the lake
And them bear cubs playing around.

When we've lighted the camp fire, fixed some grub,
Fat pork with beans from a tin.
And got both *cameras* loaded again,
I'll be mighty glad to turn in!

G. BRIGGS

KING OF STRING

One thing to which I cling
Like anything
Is string.

I save short pieces, long pieces,
Weak pieces, strong pieces,
Coarse stuff and fine stuff,
Card stuff and twine stuff.

I pick it up, scoop it up,
Twist it up, loop it up,
Make balls of it, skeins of it,
Long, knotted chains of it.

Yes, string is my dish,
And, frankly, I wish,
When it's time to unwind it,
I could find it.

RICHARD ARMOUR

PHOTOGRAPHY
HELPS THE ARCHAEOLOGIST

by

EDWARD PYDDOKE

ARCHAEOLOGICAL digging involves the destruction of a source of information, therefore the need for making a photographic record at all stages of any excavation is of vital importance. If the archaeologist's interpretation of his finds should prove to be wrong, then at least there will be photos from which a more correct assessment can be attempted. The services of a competent photographer who is aware of the special needs of archaeology are always in demand.

Let me first emphasize that what is wanted is *an accurate photographic record*, not necessarily an artistic picture: complicated shadow patterns, frame-works of leaves and so forth often serve to confuse. A clear record only is needed. Developing, printing and processing generally can follow normal procedure. Glossy black-and-white prints are essential for reproduction as illustrations. Subjects, ranging from landscapes to close-up details of coins and cathedral cornices, are nearly all stationary so there is no need for expensive camera equipment with high-speed shutters and wide-aperture lenses. For archaeological work there is nothing to beat the old-fashioned hand-and-stand or field camera. With this type of camera one is able to secure really sharp pictures by using a ground-glass focusing screen.

There are also other advantages:

(*a*) It has usually a double or triple extension focusing rack, which enables the one lens to be used for both general views and close-ups.

(*b*) Quite often the lens panel is so arranged that for special tasks the normal lens can be removed and be replaced by a wide-angle or long-focus lens.

(*c*) Such cameras normally have a rising and swinging front so that, for instance, the tops of buildings can be included in a picture without resorting to tipping the camera, which distorts vertical lines and produces an *inaccurate* record.

125

(*d*) Single plates can be exposed and developed straight away, thus allowing for the photographer to take a second picture if the first is not satisfactory. (By using an old-fashioned changing bag and a developing tank one can often dispense with the use of a dark-room so far as the development of negatives is concerned.)

Because subjects are stationary there is no need to use very fast film. A slower, fine-grain film is preferable. For the same reason there is often no need for a mechanical shutter and long exposures can be made using a lens cap only, but the direction of lighting is of first importance. The shallowest engraving will show up clearly in the photographer's studio if he arranges for his spot-light beam to strike the subject of his picture at a sufficiently acute angle. In the open-air, however, it is a matter of waiting for the sun to move round to the appropriate point; then the opportunity must be grasped or a delay of at least twenty-four hours may be incurred.

There have been many archaeological discoveries as a result of an observation at the one moment during the day when the light has been at the right angle. For instance, in all the centuries that Stonehenge had been visited, first as a curiosity and then as an "ancient monument", no one had noticed or even suspected that there were ancient engravings on the standing stones until, in 1953, R. J. C. Atkinson looked into his focusing screen and saw what appeared to be a carving of a Bronze Age axe! Subsequent close inspection of the stones themselves has shown that there are in fact many shallow carvings of axes, daggers and other objects.

When a subject has been so placed as to be permanently in shadow and sheltered from the sun it has happened that photographs have been taken even by moonlight. When Dr. E. C. Curwen was excavating at Whitehawk Camp near Brighton he found the winter sun too low in the sky to light the bottom of his trenches, but a high full moon shone right down into them. Long exposures were obviously necessary.

As another example of the importance of lighting, Roman villas and even whole towns buried below the earth and invisible from ground level, have shown up in photographs from the air. There is no magic in aerial photography: the explanation is that it has sometimes happened that an air-photograph has been taken just when the sun's rays have been throwing shadows behind banks and depressions so slight as to be unnoticed from the ground. A vertical photograph, also helps to show the shape and plan of things which are meaningless when seen obliquely.

A dusting of fine powdery snow blown along the surface of the ground will also sometimes settle in depressions so shallow as to have remained unnoticed from ground-level.

Other discoveries have been made as the result of air-photographs showing up (because of the favourable view-point) sites whose only surface indication has been a slight variation in the colouring of, say, a crop of corn. Where there are footings of walls below the ground surface the corn's roots penetrate less deeply than those of the corn on either side, and the grain ripens sooner. On the other hand, where filled-in ditches allow corn roots to penetrate more deeply than elsewhere the plants will find extra moisture and remain green longer than others.

The Use of Colour Filters

Such slight differences in colour can sometimes also be seen from the ground. In either case it is for the photographer to use such film, or plate emulsion, as will emphasize and show up these differences. He can further emphasize the differences by the use of colour filters fixed before his lens; he is justified even in securing a much exaggerated rendering provided he produces a record otherwise accurate. The same exaggeration may be necessary to show up such slight differences in colour as exist between the various layers of earth which show in the sides of an excavation trench.

To secure an accurate picture from the air the photograph must be taken vertically and not obliquely, for perspective distorts photographs taken at an angle. For the same reason the archaeologist tries always, if it is at all possible, to take his photographs along a line which is at right-angles to the surface of his subject. So as to make his record complete he will also always place a scale alongside the object he is photographing. Obviously unless a scale is shown it may be impossible to judge from a picture of a single simple pottery vessel whether it is three inches or three feet high, and the scale must lie in a plane parallel to that of the photographic film.

The scale usually used with small objects and in the studio is a length of card marked on one side in inches and on the other in centimetres. For outdoor work concerned with banks, ditches and trenches, walling and so on, a very common scale is the surveyor's familiar ranging pole, which is painted red, white and black in one-foot divisions. Human figures must be avoided and are useful only to give an approximate scale when one is photographing large sections of extensive structures such as castles and hill-forts.

In the studio much time has to be spent in preparing photographs of the excavator's "small finds"—brooches, coins, pottery fragments, flint blades and so on. Skill in lighting is needed to bring out the details required. To avoid excessive shadows the photographer will sometimes place his objects on a suspended sheet of ground glass. During a long exposure one or more spot-lights illuminate the top surfaces; another is waved slowly on to a reflector below so that some light comes up through the glass and provides a light background for the picture.

Three kinds of photographic work occasionally used are:

(a) When Stone Age engraved pictures on bone implements have been so shallow as to cast almost no shadow even with the most highly angled lighting or have been on bones whose over-curvature produced a shadow, a fluorescent powder has sometimes been dusted on and then brushed off everywhere but where it has remained in the engraving. A photograph has then been taken by ultra-violet light which made the remaining powder glow against a dark background.

(b) The second special form of photography is that using infra-red light with special plates and filters. This gives some power of penetration and can sometimes be used for recording faded writing even below words which have been written later on the same paper or parchment.

(c) Finally there is the X-ray photograph which requires special and rather dangerous equipment. In the same way that a surgeon photographs broken bones and an art gallery examines paintings for faking and over-painting, the archaeologist records the existence, for instance, of traces of silver inlay in a very rusty iron sword or buckle.

"This will give 'em something to think about one day!"

PLATE 6. Archaeology tells a grim story of battle; a Roman arrowhead is seen embedded in the spine of a defender of Maiden Castle, Dorset. (Below) A photographer at work in an excavation trench.

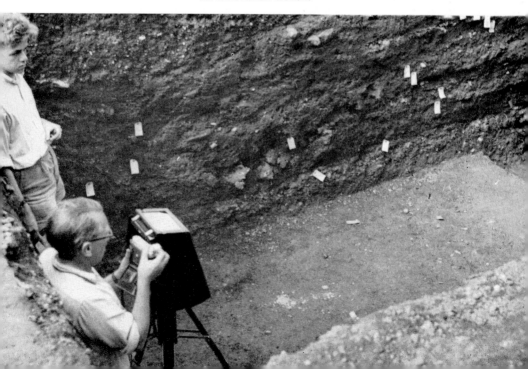

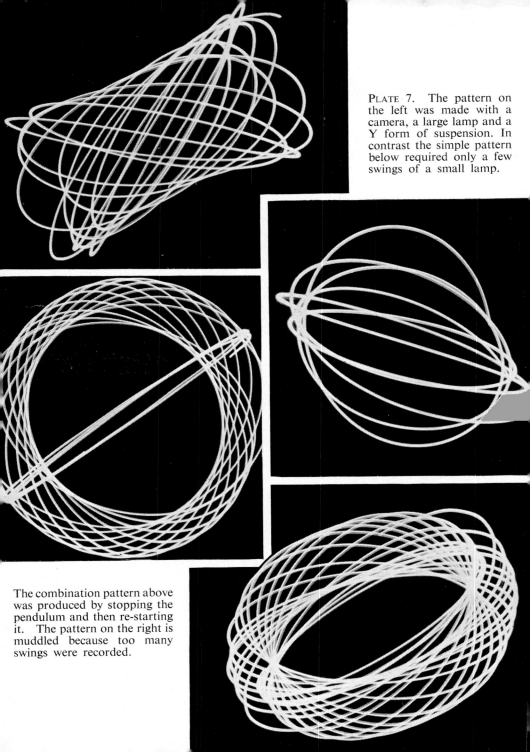

PLATE 7. The pattern on the left was made with a camera, a large lamp and a Y form of suspension. In contrast the simple pattern below required only a few swings of a small lamp.

The combination pattern above was produced by stopping the pendulum and then re-starting it. The pattern on the right is muddled because too many swings were recorded.

DESIGNS FROM YOUR CAMERA

A<small>N</small> unlimited number of different designs like those reproduced opposite can be made by anyone owning a camera, no matter how simple it is. The cheapest box camera works well, provided it is fitted with a close-up lens to ensure good definition in the lines of the patterns. The varied patterns are made by placing the camera on the floor with the lens pointing vertically upwards at a pendulum, at the lower end of which is a small electric lamp. The pendulum is set swinging and the shutter of the camera is opened and allowed to remain open for as long as is thought necessary to produce a pattern. The moving light source produces a narrow trace on the film which is almost black in the negative and hence white in the print. By a suitable technique the pattern can be converted to one of black lines on a white background in the print.

The pendulum is merely a suitable length of thin cord or very strong thread and the weight at the bottom is provided by a 4½-volt, three-cell flat torch battery with brass strips for connections. The lamp is also one intended for a torch and should be designed for 3·5 volts with a miniature Edison screw cap. A lamp with a tiny coiled filament will give a finer trace than one with an *S* filament. The patterns with rather thick lines shown were made with a lamp having a fairly large filament in order to give bold lines that would reproduce clearly. In general a pattern of fine lines is more pleasing.

A lampholder suitable for the lamp used is fixed to the battery by means of adhesive tape and it is connected to the brass strips of the battery by two short lengths of insulated wire. Ideally the connections should be soldered as any poor contacts in the circuit may cause the lamp to flicker and the lines of any patterns will be weak or broken in places. There is no need to provide a switch for controlling the lamp as it can be switched off by loosening it slightly in its holder.

The length of the pendulum will govern its period of swing and an overall length of about 4 feet will be found suitable. When it is at rest

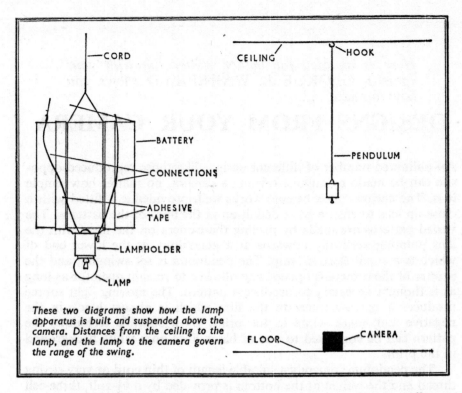

These two diagrams show how the lamp apparatus is built and suspended above the camera. Distances from the ceiling to the lamp, and the lamp to the camera govern the range of the swing.

the lamp will be about 4 feet from the camera lens assuming an ordinary room with a ceiling about 8 feet high. Some means has to be found for supporting the pendulum and it is usually possible to insert a small screw eye or hook in the ceiling, taking care not to crack the plaster. As the camera shutter is left open for many seconds while recording the movement of the lamp, it is essential that the room shall be capable of being darkened, otherwise pictures of the ceiling will be obtained as well as a pattern and the background will not be black in the print. The tiny lamp on the end of the pendulum gives enough light to see by so that the camera can be operated without falling over the furniture!

Use a medium-speed film with the lens aperture at f/11. Too slow a film gives only a faint trace, difficult to print, and a very fast film may cause light scatter on the emulsion. Try to record the first attempt on the last frame of a film which has been used for other subjects, then if the result is not satisfactory adjustments can be made before using a new film. The only adjustments possible with box cameras with fixed lens apertures are to vary the film speed or change the power of the lamp used on the pendulum.

If the pendulum is made to swing widely it may go right out of the field of view of the lens to begin with, but it is an easy matter to work out how much swing is required to keep the lamp in the picture. If the bottom of the pendulum is 4 feet from the lens and the camera is a $2\frac{1}{4} \times 3\frac{1}{4}$ inch instrument with a 4-inch lens then a swing of the pendulum 2 feet wide will be imaged on the film as 2 inches—within the picture space with a little to spare. A $2\frac{1}{4}$-inch square camera is likely to have a 3-inch lens with which a 2-foot swing will be reproduced as $1\frac{1}{2}$ inches on the film.

Mark the floor in some way so that the camera can be replaced in exactly the same place every time the film is wound on from one exposure to the next. Switch on the lamp by screwing it home firmly in its holder and set the pendulum swinging. Initially it may jerk about a little but it will settle down to a regular motion quite quickly. Turn out the room lights and open the camera shutter which should have been set to its *B* position beforehand. The focus has been set for the distance of the lamp from the camera, or in the case of a simple camera with no means of focusing, the close-up lens has been brought into use. The number of swings the pendulum is allowed to make will determine the complexity of the pattern. Try about ten swings to start with and then perhaps smaller and larger numbers. When enough have been recorded the camera shutter is closed and the film wound on immediately. Great variety can be obtained by holding a piece of card over the lens after a few swings, stopping the pendulum, and setting it swinging again, recording a few more swings. This can be repeated several times if desired but very complicated patterns are apt to look muddled.

Reversing the Print

More varieties of patterns can be obtained by suspending the pendulum in the form of a letter Y. The leg of the Y should be made about the same length as the V portion. If this is done two hooks will be needed in the ceiling between 2 and 3 feet apart. A further variation may be obtained by having the lamp and holder only on the pendulum and supplying the current from a battery via a thin twin flex running down the pendulum cord. In fact, thin flex may well serve as a pendulum. A weight will be required to take the place of the battery and this can be any convenient object having a symmetrical shape and of about the same weight as the battery. A switch is now incorporated in the circuit and with its aid patterns of dotted and dashed lines can be made. Also, composite patterns can be made by switching off the lamp for a time during the swinging of the pendulum and then switching it on again.

It is not essential to have the camera directly underneath the pendulum; it can be pointed obliquely upwards which introduces perspective into the patterns. Focusing is now a little more difficult and it may be as well to stop the lens down further to ensure sufficient depth of field, using a faster film if necessary. A film devoted entirely to these pictures should be developed for a little longer than usual—say 20 per cent—to make sure of strong lines that will print as perfectly white on an absolutely black background. To produce prints in which the lines are black on a white ground involves printing the original negatives on to sheet "process" film by contact and developing this fully in a contrasty developer. The result will be a positive consisting of clear lines on a very dark background. Under-exposure of the positive will give a background that is not black enough and over-exposure will cause the fine lines of the pattern to clog. Process film is obtainable through a photographic dealer in all sizes.

WIMSEY.

CHESS PROBLEMS

set by

JOHN BEE

No. 1

Black, 10 pieces

White, 11 pieces
White to play and win

No. 2

Black, 10 pieces

White, 10 pieces
In positions like this a small advantage
is sufficient to win. Black moves, and
gains a pawn. How?

No. 3

Black, 12 pieces

White, 12 pieces
Black has played P–R3. What is White's
reply?

No. 4

Black, 13 pieces

White, 13 pieces
White to play: what is the continuation?

(Solutions on page 192)

OUT OF THE NIGHT

by
COLIN ROBERTSON

This ONE-ACT PLAY for five male characters has a running time of 20 minutes. It is ideal for a Christmas party play-reading or as an item in a Youth Club concert or Scout show. Written permission must be obtained from The Editor, Boy's Own Paper (see page 6) before it can be performed in public, including charity performances.

Characters: MR. REDMAYNE
FORBES, a chauffeur
MR. PEPPER
DETECTIVE-SERGEANT PARKER
DETECTIVE-INSPECTOR DAVIS

Scene: MR. PEPPER'S *office in London.*

Time: *The present. A winter's evening.*
The only essential articles of furniture are a desk, with a telephone and lamp on it; a desk-chair; a waste-paper basket; a safe—which might be a wooden

*box painted appropriately. There is a door facing the
desk, and one corner of the room is curtained off.
When the CURTAIN rises, the lights, including the
desk-lamp, are lit.* MR. REDMAYNE, *a handsome man
wearing a well-cut dark overcoat, a silk scarf, and
gloves, is standing near the desk. He picks up his
black felt hat lying there and flicks a speck of dust
from it before putting it down again farther away
from some business papers. He is casting an eye over
these, his lips pursed, when there is a tap on the door.*

REDMAYNE: [*looking up quickly*] Is that you, Forbes?
FORBES: [*off*] Yes, sir.

> REDMAYNE *goes to the door and admits him.*
> FORBES *is wearing a chauffeur's uniform and
> cap. He looks ill at ease.*

I've brought the car round from the mews, sir.
REDMAYNE: Always punctual, eh, Forbes?
FORBES: Lady Manley's party begins at——
REDMAYNE: [*interrupting*] Yes, I know. And she hates her
guests to be late. But on this occasion——

> *He breaks off with a thin smile.*

FORBES: [*glancing about the office*] I didn't expect to find
you alone.
REDMAYNE: I'll explain later. Not now.
FORBES: It's a perishing cold night. [*He rubs his hands to-
gether.*] Will you be much longer, sir?
REDMAYNE: Not very long. I've still a little business to attend to.
FORBES: [*nods*] I'll wait in the car.
REDMAYNE: If I don't join you in ten minutes you might phone
Lady Manley from the call box across the road.
Tell her I've been delayed and offer my apologies.
FORBES: [*somewhat reluctantly*] If you think it's necessary,
sir. But——
REDMAYNE: [*interrupting*] Politeness demands it, Forbes.
FORBES: Very well.
REDMAYNE: If I phone her myself she'll probably chatter away
as she usually does. [*As* FORBES *nods.*] Now do as
I say.

135

FORBES: [*uneasily*] I hope you won't be much longer, that's all.

> *He moves to the door.* REDMAYNE *glances at a newspaper lying near the end of the desk. He picks it up, tapping it with his forefinger.*

REDMAYNE: Er—just a moment. Listen to this.

FORBES: [*fretfully*] Look, sir——!

REDMAYNE: [*blandly*] There's no violent hurry. Don't *worry*, Forbes. If I leave a few minutes later it won't make much difference.

> *He refers to the newspaper again.*

This is interesting. That fellow, Velvetfoot has made the headlines. [*Reading aloud:*] "Master cracksman busy again."

FORBES: [*impatiently*] I saw it in my own paper.

REDMAYNE: You did, eh? You should have told me. It seems Mrs. Culton's pearls were stolen last night. [*He reads silently for a few moments,* FORBES *shifting from one foot to the other.*] H'm. . . . The police are convinced it was Velvetfoot's handiwork. And listen to this—he sent her a letter saying he was going to steal them!

> FORBES *looks anxiously at his wrist-watch.*

FORBES: It's after seven!

> REDMAYNE *ignores this reminder.*

REDMAYNE: [*musingly*] You know, I believe Lady Manley invited Mrs. Culton to the party to-night. . . .I wonder if she'll be there?

FORBES: [*despairingly*] Does it matter? Look——

REDMAYNE: If she is, I've no doubt she'll have a lot to say about the robbery. I should like to hear the details.

FORBES: [*muttering*] If we ever get there!

REDMAYNE: Such impatience! We shall, Forbes, we shall. All right, off you go. [*As* FORBES *is about to open the door.*] And don't come badgering me again, there's a good chap—even if I'm much longer than you expect. I'll finish my business as soon as I can.

136

FORBES *nods, and exits.* REDMAYNE *tosses the newspaper back on to the desk, drums his fingers on the edge reflectively, then sits down in the desk-chair. He opens one of the drawers, glances inside, and closes it again, opening another drawer. He takes a single sheet of writing paper from it. We realize it is a letter as he unfolds it and reads it.*

REDMAYNE: [*muttering the words*] "I propose to pay you a visit shortly. It is, I think, unnecessary to state the nature of my business, since my name is—Velvet-foot."

With a reflective expression, REDMAYNE *crushes the letter slowly in his hand, and drops it into the waste-paper basket. He is turning back to the desk again when the door opens suddenly and a man darts in. He is shabbily dressed and is pointing a gun in his jacket pocket, his whole attitude tense.*

INTRUDER:	Don't move!
REDMAYNE:	[*frowning*] What's the meaning of this? Who are you?
INTRUDER:	[*sourly*] Think I'm going to tell you my name? Not likely! After I've got what I want I hope we shall never meet again.
REDMAYNE:	I'm beginning to wish we had never met at all! Is that a gun you've got there?
INTRUDER:	[*curtly*] Want to see it?
REDMAYNE:	No, I'll take your word for it.
INTRUDER:	[*sourly*] Maybe we'll get along fine.
REDMAYNE:	I doubt it. What do you want? [*The man's eyes dart towards the safe.*]
INTRUDER:	Can't you guess?
REDMAYNE:	Money, eh?
INTRUDER:	What else, Mr. Pepper.
REDMAYNE:	So you know my name.
INTRUDER:	I know the name under which you run your business: "Henry Pepper and Company." I saw it on the brass plate outside the front door. But I sneaked in the back way, see? That lock was easy to pick.
REDMAYNE:	[*acidly*] So it seems. Surely you're not Velvetfoot?
INTRUDER:	You mean—— Me? Not on your life.
REDMAYNE:	No, I thought not. He's some pretensions to being a gentleman, they say. I can't imagine him stooping to a crude hold-up like this.
INTRUDER:	[*frowning*] I'll get what I came for, all right. [*Sharply as* REDMAYNE *moves slightly.*] Stay put— or I'll put a bullet through you!
REDMAYNE:	I really believe you might.
INTRUDER:	Keep thinking that. [*Pause.*] I've picked my time— I know we shan't be disturbed.
REDMAYNE:	You're sadly mistaken. My chauffeur will be back——
INTRUDER:	[*interrupting*] No—you told him to stop badgering you.
REDMAYNE:	[*surprised*] Oh?
INTRUDER:	After ten minutes or so he'll ring your friend Lady Manley. Then he'll sit in the car waiting for you— that's all.

138

REDMAYNE:	You must be clairvoyant!
INTRUDER:	I was listening outside the door. I sneaked in earlier, see? Just before he came. I heard every word.
REDMAYNE:	H'm . . . You were lucky.
INTRUDER:	Which means you're going to be very *unlucky*.
REDMAYNE:	Perhaps. Nevertheless, I think you're taking a big risk, my friend. As soon as you've gone I shall phone the police.
INTRUDER:	[*sneeringly*] And then?
REDMAYNE:	They'll track you down.
INTRUDER:	Not if I know it! The cops always look for a motive. But just consider, Mr. Pepper—I don't bear you a grudge. I've never seen you before in my life. There's nothing to connect us. I came out of the night, and I shall vanish into it again—leaving no clues behind. [*Grimly.*] I'll see to that.
REDMAYNE:	Yes, I follow your argument. But there's just one thing I'd like to point out.
INTRUDER:	Well?
REDMAYNE:	[*emphatically*] You won't leave with *my* money.
INTRUDER:	No? That's what *you* think. [*He moves nearer the desk. Then curtly:*] Stand up—and no tricks mind.

REDMAYNE *shrugs. Unhurriedly, he gets to his feet.*

REDMAYNE:	Now what?
INTRUDER:	Put up your hands. [REDMAYNE *obeys.*] We'll see what you've got in your pockets.
INTRUDER:	You can keep 'em—just chicken feed.

He steps warily up to REDMAYNE, *tapping the pockets of his overcoat.*

Okay. Now unbutton it.

REDMAYNE:	I suppose I must. [*He does so.*]
INTRUDER:	Up with your hands again.

After REDMAYNE *has raised them, the man taps the pockets of his jacket and trousers.*

No gun.

REDMAYNE:	I'm a law-abiding citizen. Did you really think I carried one!

139

INTRUDER:	The key to your safe. Where is it?

> REDMAYNE *shrugs. He takes a key-ring from his trousers' pocket, holding up the keys with a cynical expression. The other snatches them from him, steps back, and peers at them, frowning.*

	It isn't here.
REDMAYNE:	[*sardonically*] Did I say it was?
INTRUDER:	Stop acting, will you?
REDMAYNE:	Now, I imagine, you'll search me much more thoroughly. But you won't find it. Go ahead.
INTRUDER:	[*scowling*] Why won't I find it?
REDMAYNE:	Because I don't carry it on me. [*Smiles mockingly.*] A precautionary measure. But carry on—amuse yourself.
INTRUDER:	[*grimly*] I don't find this funny.
REDMAYNE:	[*dryly*] To be perfectly frank, neither do I.

> *The man raises the gun threateningly in his pocket, scowling.*

INTRUDER:	Where do you keep it? You're going to tell me.
REDMAYNE:	[*firmly*] I think not.
INTRUDER:	It's somewhere in this office. Must be.
REDMAYNE:	[*dryly*] For one so crude you're pretty bright.

> *The man moves quickly up behind him, jabbing the gun savagely into the small of his back.*

INTRUDER:	Tell me, or else——!

> REDMAYNE *remains silent.*

INTRUDER:	[*stridently*] Go on—talk!

> *We see that* REDMAYNE *is more than worried, forcing himself to speak calmly.*

REDMAYNE:	There's no need to raise your voice. I can hear you.
INTRUDER:	You'll hear a bullet, too, unless——
REDMAYNE:	What good will that do you? To open the safe you need the key. I'm not going to tell you where it is.
INTRUDER:	We'll see!

REDMAYNE: [*quickly*] I suggest you look for it instead of shooting me. If you consider a moment I'm sure you'll agree.

INTRUDER: Shut up! I've listened to you long enough. You're a pretty smooth talker.

REDMAYNE: It's my only weapon. You have me at a disadvantage. But I would remind you, my friend, that armed robbery is a far more serious offence than mere larceny. Think it over. [*Short pause.*] When you burst in here with that gun you didn't expect I should prove so difficult. And now you're letting you're—er—enthusiasm run away with your judgment.

INTRUDER: I'm smart enough.

REDMAYNE: In that case you'll stop talking all this dangerous nonsense about shooting me. Dangerous for you as well as for me. Suppose the police do catch you. What then?

The man hesitates, staring at him sullenly.

INTRUDER: Move round to the other side of the desk. Go on.

REDMAYNE: Very well. [*He obeys.*]

INTRUDER: [*sharply*] That's far enough!

REDMAYNE *halts, facing the desk-chair. The man pushes it out of the way, and keeping him covered, opens one drawer after another, searching with growing impatience. Finally, he darts round the desk towards* REDMAYNE.

INTRUDER: [*breathing heavily*] Maybe you were bluffing. Maybe you've got the key on you. We'll see! Empty your pockets.

REDMAYNE: Really! Is that necessary?

INTRUDER: You heard me. Get on with it. Put the stuff on the desk.

REDMAYNE *shrugs. He takes various objects from his pockets, including a wallet, a handkerchief, a fountain pen, cigarette-case and lighter, and some small change, placing them on the desk.*

141

REDMAYNE:	That's all, I think.
INTRUDER:	[*grimly*] You think! I'll make sure in a minute. Stand back, and put your hands up again.

> *He waits until* REDMAYNE *has done so, then opens the cigarette-case quickly, snaps it shut, puts it down again, and opens the wallet, feeling tentatively inside. He scowls, tossing it back on the desk.*

REDMAYNE:	Satisfied?
INTRUDER:	Not yet.

> *He steps up to* REDMAYNE *warily, and dips exploring fingers into his waistcoat pockets. He finds nothing there.*

Turn out your trouser pockets.

> REDMAYNE *complies, exhibiting the linings.*

REDMAYNE:	Pity you didn't take my word for it.

> *Suddenly he brings his hand down and across, sweeping the other's gun aside. He seizes him and there is a brief struggle. But the man tears himself loose, leaping back out of reach.*

INTRUDER:	[*furious*] Try that again and I'll let you have it. . . . The key—where is it?
REDMAYNE:	[*curtly*] Find out.
INTRUDER:	If you don't tell me by heaven I'll——!
REDMAYNE:	[*quickly*] So you're determined to shoot me! Either you shoot to wound or to kill. I can't believe you would commit murder. If on the other hand——
INTRUDER:	Shut up, will you! I've wasted enough time.
REDMAYNE:	The way you're going on you'll waste a lot more —in prison. And all you'll get for your bullet is the few pounds in my wallet. Is it really worth it?
INTRUDER:	You'll talk.
REDMAYNE:	No.
INTRUDER:	All right, you've asked for it. I'll count three. If you don't change your mind before then—I'm not kidding, I mean it.

His whole attitude suggests he does.

One . . .!

REDMAYNE, *desperate now, licks his lips.*

REDMAYNE: The shot will make quite a noise. My chauffeur will hear it.

INTRUDER: No. You forget, Mr. Pepper. This is a big building —besides, your office faces a side street. [*Implacably.*] Two . . .!

A dramatic pause.

REDMAYNE: [*bitter reluctance*] All right—you win.

He has barely spoken when the telephone rings. Both of them glance sharply towards it.

Ah! [*With considerable relief.*] In the nick of time!

INTRUDER: What do you mean?

REDMAYNE: Simply that I was expecting the call.

INTRUDER: [*his eyes narrowed*] You were?

REDMAYNE: From Detective-Inspector Davis.

INTRUDER: I don't believe it.

REDMAYNE: You can believe what you like. He said he would phone me shortly after seven. I was waiting for the call when you came in.

INTRUDER: You mean—your unfinished business?

REDMAYNE: Yes. You see, I was expecting a visit from a much more accomplished thief than yourself—Velvetfoot. If I don't answer the phone, well—— [*He shrugged significantly.*]

INTRUDER: He'll think there's something wrong.

REDMAYNE: He will. How much longer are you going to let it ring?

The man chews his lip undecidedly. Then:

INTRUDER: Answer it. Put him off. [*Menacingly.*] One word out of place and I'll shoot.

REDMAYNE *picks up the phone.*

143

REDMAYNE: [*to phone*] Pepper here. . . . No, nothing unusual has happened so far, Inspector. . . . Yes. . . . Yes, by all means. It might be safer. Good-bye. [*He replaces the phone.*]

INTRUDER: What did he say?

REDMAYNE looks at him with a mocking smile.

REDMAYNE: He wanted to see me. He said he'd join me here as soon as possible. Naturally, I didn't try to stop him.

INTRUDER: You're lying—another bluff.

REDMAYNE: [*confidently*] No, my friend. Fate is against you. Now don't you think you'd better make yourself scarce—before you are arrested?

The man glowers at him suspiciously.

REDMAYNE: [*continues*] If he jumps in a police car he could be here in less than five minutes. So you'd better make up your mind quickly.

The man still hesitates.

Stay by all means, if you want to. Nothing would please me better—now!

The man sidles balefully to the door, opens it, and darts out. REDMAYNE *breathes a sigh deep of relief. He looks at his wrist-watch then pockets his personal possessions lying on the desk. Pausing a moment he pats the telephone affectionately, smiling to himself.*

Thanks—that was a pretty close shave.

He walks smartly to that part of the office which is curtained off, flinging the curtain aside. As he does so we see a middle-aged man there. He has been bound to a chair, and gagged. REDMAYNE *eyes him quizzically.*

Did you find it amusing? No, I see you didn't. These crude amateurs! [*He clicks his tongue deprecatingly.*] They've a lot to learn. Don't you agree—Mr. Pepper?

144

As MR. PEPPER *stares at him helplessly, he goes on:*

I hope we shan't be interrupted again. Er—in case you're interested, that call was simply a wrong number. So we shan't have the pleasure of seeing Inspector Davis, after all. [*Chuckles.*] He'd give a lot to get his hands on me. [*Quoting mockingly.*] "Velvetfoot—audacious cracksman arrested!" But tonight I am afraid I must disappoint him again. Now, if you don't mind, I'll take the key to your safe.

He thrusts his hand into MR. PEPPER'S *trousers' pocket, brings out a key ring, and detaches one of the keys. He goes to the safe, unlocks it, and bending down on one knee helps himself to the notes inside, transferring them quickly to his pockets. Finally, he returns to* MR. PEPPER, *flicking some of the notes before his impotent gaze.*

REDMAYNE: [*continues*] Good-bye, Mr. Pepper. I really must be going now.

> *Smiling, he crosses to the desk, picks up his hat and puts it on unhurriedly. Then he goes to the door, switching off the light. Most of the office is in deep shadow now, the lamp throwing a pool of light on to the desk. He is about to open the door when someone taps on it. Stiffening, he backs towards the desk.*
>
> *The door opens slowly. For a few moments we are kept in suspense. Then we see the chauffeur's uniform as he steps in, remaining near the door, his face hidden by the gloom.*

Oh, it's you, Forbes! [*Releasing his breath.*] Phew!

> *Actually, it is not* FORBES, *but we are also deceived.*

IMPERSONATOR: Sorry if I startled you, sir.

REDMAYNE: [*sharply*] I told you to wait in the car.

> *The other turns his head towards* MR. PEPPER, *then back again to* REDMAYNE.

IMPERSONATOR: I got a bit worried. Is everything all right?

REDMAYNE: [*nods*] In a way it's a pity you didn't return sooner.

IMPERSONATOR: Oh? Why?

REDMAYNE: I had a visitor—quite a tough customer. He sneaked in with a gun soon after you left. Believe it or not he came to rob the safe!

IMPERSONATOR: [*apparent anxiety*] What?

REDMAYNE: I had a devil of a job to get rid of him. Fortunately the phone rang while I was getting the worst of the argument. It was a wrong number, but I convinced him it was Inspector Davis and that he would be here in a few minutes. After that he decided to leave—rather hurriedly.

IMPERSONATOR: [*admiringly*] You are a one, sir!

REDMAYNE: [*smugly*] I don't think I did too badly, myself. [*He walked round the desk, coming more into the light.*] The Velvetfoot technique, Forbes.

IMPERSONATOR:	You've got the money?
REDMAYNE:	[*tapping his pockets*] Right here.
IMPERSONATOR:	Then we'd better get out—quick.
REDMAYNE:	[*chidingly*] My dear chap, you're always in such a hurry. The man's gone. He slipped out by the back door, I expect. That's the way he came in.
IMPERSONATOR:	But the police! They might show up——
REDMAYNE:	[*interrupting*] They might. There is always that possibility. That's just what appeals to me—the risks I take.
IMPERSONATOR:	[*balefully*] Maybe too many. I'm in this too, sir!
REDMAYNE:	Surely you've worked with me long enough to know that you've greatly overestimated the intelligence of the police. Really, Forbes, I'm disappointed in you.

He looks down at the desk, drums his fingers on it, and looks up again.

As it happened I hadn't taken the key to the safe from our friend Mr. Pepper when this rough character interrupted me. You need luck in this game.

The IMPERSONATOR *speaks grimly in his own voice.*

IMPERSONATOR:	And yours has run out, Velvetfoot!

He switches on the room light.

REDMAYNE:	[*startled recognition*] Inspector Davis!

The INSPECTOR *walks up to him.*

INSPECTOR DAVIS:	Y—es. I've been looking forward to this for years. Kind of you to tell me you'd actually got the money. Now we've caught you red-handed.
REDMAYNE:	[*scowling*] We? You mean——

He looks towards MR. PEPPER.

INSPECTOR DAVIS:	[*shakes his head*] Not entirely—though Mr. Pepper got in touch with us as soon as he received your letter. This time we had everything laid on— Sergeant Parker and myself.

147

REDMAYNE: [*puzzled*] Sergeant Parker?

INSPECTOR DAVIS: [*nods*] We were waiting for you in this building. We—er—detained your accomplice, Forbes, after he left to return to your car.

He walks towards MR. PEPPER.

Sorry, I had to let him tie you up, sir. I expect you thought we'd fallen down on the job. We'll soon have you free——

Seizing his opportunity, REDMAYNE *makes a dash for the door—only to be confronted on the threshold by the man we saw earlier—the supposed burglar.* REDMAYNE *starts back in astonishment.*

REDMAYNE: You!

DAVIS: [*smiling grimly*] Sergeant Parker. [*To* PARKER.] All right, Parker, I'll take care of him. Release Mr. Pepper.

SERGEANT PARKER: Yes, sir.

He crosses toward him and sets to work as INSPECTOR DAVIS *confronts* REDMAYNE *again.*

INSPECTOR DAVIS: [*sardonically*] You look surprised.

REDMAYNE: [*grudgingly*] You're much smarter than I thought, Inspector.

INSPECTOR DAVIS: Thank you.

REDMAYNE: [*sourly*] Parker has missed his vocation—he should have been an actor.

SERGEANT PARKER *looks round with a satisfied grin.*

But I don't quite understand why he was so anxious to get the key?

INSPECTOR DAVIS: Ah that! At the time we didn't know whether you'd opened the safe or not. From the way you spoke to Forbes we assumed you hadn't. We had to be sure.

REDMAYNE: I *see*—so that you could arrest me with the loot actually in my possession.

INSPECTOR DAVIS:	Just so. Parker wasn't really interested in the key. His object was to search you without arousing your suspicions.
REDMAYNE:	[*sourly*] He made a very thorough job of it!
INSPECTOR DAVIS:	[*smiling thinly*] Yes. If he hadn't, you might have guessed he wasn't what he appeared to be. [*Dryly.*] We didn't underestimate *your* intelligence. So he had to continue in the role longer than was strictly necessary. If you'd had the money on you I should have joined him at once, of course.
REDMAYNE:	[*with a touch of his former bravado*] You think of everthing, Inspector.
INSPECTOR DAVIS:	[*sternly*] Take the notes out of your pockets and put them on the desk.

> *While* REDMAYNE *is doing so,* MR. PEPPER, *now released, steps angrily up to him.*

MR. PEPPER:	You scoundrel!

> *He looks as if he is about to strike* REDMAYNE *when* INSPECTOR DAVIS *turns to him restrainingly.*

INSPECTOR DAVIS:	Now, sir! Leave him to us—the law will deal with him. [*To* REDMAYNE.] You've had a pretty long innings, Velvetfoot.
REDMAYNE:	Y—es. It's a great pity though—Lady Manley will be *so* disappointed. . . . All right, Inspector, I'm ready.

> SERGEANT PARKER *begins to lead him away.* INSPECTOR DAVIS *stares after them then down at the notes as:*

THE CURTAIN FALLS

LAUGH
WITH
B.O.P!

"It's for my master—he's lost his voice"

"But why not, mother? Flies do it!"

"Keep quiet—maybe they'll think we're out!"

"Got it—the phrase book says it means
'we are friends' "

CLEW

"Don't you dare take my school report and rip
it to shreds before my dad sees it!"

TRAVEL BY RAIL

"Porter!"

MOSE.

WIMSEY.

"Be kind but firm—that's my motto!"

MAKE THE B.O.P DINGHY

Designed by P. W. BLANDFORD

ONE of the cheapest constructional materials today is hardboard and the oil-tempered variety is suitable for boat skins. The original boat was built from oil-tempered Royal Board at a total cost of about £5. Standard sheets are 8 ft. by 4 ft. by $\frac{1}{8}$ in. and this dinghy is the longest that can be built without joints. It is a general-purpose boat, suitable for use under oars or an outboard motor up to $1\frac{1}{2}$ h.p. It will comfortably carry a crew of three and a reasonable amount of kit, and will float in 6 in. of water.

Construction is simple. There are no jigs or formers to make. The boat does not have to be set up for long periods, and it can be packed away between working periods. Two boys, with the average handyman's tool kit, should be able to build the boat in about thirty working hours. Do not use ordinary hardboard—it must be oil-tempered. The wood may be any reasonably straight-grained softwood, or a mild hardwood, such as mahogany. In the original boat, most of the parts were parana pine. All joints should be glued, with a synthetic resin glue (such as Aerolite 306 or Cascamite One-shot) and screwed or nailed. Make the transom (A) and bow board (B) first (Fig. 1). Plane the edges to the angles shown. The angles at the sides may need adjusting later, but planing before assembly is easier. The top edges are rounded in cross section.

To mark out the shape of the bottom, draw a line 20 in. from one edge of a sheet and draw lines across it at 12 in. intervals and one at 82 in. Use the half plan (Fig. 2) to make distances each side of the centre line, then bend a thin piece of wood through the points and draw the curve. Support the sheet on boxes and cut around the outline with a hand-saw. Fix the transom and bow board to the ends with glue and screws at about 3 in. intervals driven from below. Use the hardboard with the smooth side outwards. Put knees (C) at the ends (Fig. 3). Drill holes in each to take rope painters. The chines (D) should be planed to the angle shown (Fig. 4) before fixing. This angle is approxi-

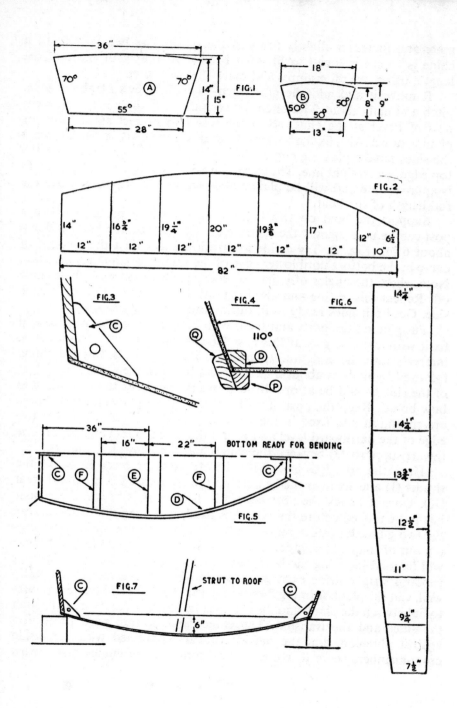

FIG.1

FIG.2

FIG.3

FIG.4

FIG.6

FIG.5

BOTTOM READY FOR BENDING

FIG.7

STRUT TO ROOF

mate and increases slightly towards the bows. The best way to fit a chine is to cut one end to fit, then bend it to shape for most of the length, using several cramps, and mark the other end.

Remove it and add the glue, then fix with screws at about 6 in. pitch and nails about 2 in. pitch between them. If there is any unevenness of bevel at the ends, allow the wood to project sufficiently for planing down. Also fix the bottom stiffeners (E and F) (Fig. 5). Although the sides have a pleasing curve when bent, the developed shape of the top edge is a straight line. The curve shown for the bottom edge (Fig. 6) is approximate and will be planed after fixing. Cut a pair of sides the full length of the boat.

Support the boat on two boxes or trestles in a position where a post can be used against the centre piece (E) to press the bottom down about 6 in. (Fig. 7). Try a side in position and adjust the amount of curve in the bottom until lower edge of the side approximately matches. Note where the angles of chines or ends are incorrect and plane them off. Repeat this testing and planing until the joints are a good fit each side. Get both sides ready to fit during one working session.

Put glue on the parts and then, with help, hold a side in place and fix it with a few screws. If this is satisfactory put screws at about 3 in. intervals into the ends and at about 6 in. intervals along the chine, followed by nails at about 2 in. intervals between them. The top edges of the side should be at or a little above the edges of the transom and bow board. Keep the post in position and fit the gunwales (G). These are sprung in and fixed in the same way as the chines. Plane the top edge of the hardboard level and round the inner edges (Fig. 8). Fix the thwart supports (J) between the chines and the gunwales (Fig. 9).

Have the aft edges level with the aft edges of piece E. Make the thwart (I) and fix it to the bearers on the supports. Fix a central strut (K). Do not knock the post out until the thwart is fitted. If the boat has to be moved before the thwart is fixed, nail a strip of wood across the two gunwales before removing the post, to prevent the sides springing out of shape. Strengthen the four corners with knees (M). As these will be used in lifting the boat, round the edges well. Put a half-round rubbing strip outside each gunwale (H—Fig. 8). Ensure it fits really well. Cut the plank forming the stern sheets (L) to fit, and make supports to fit between the plank and the chines (Fig. 10). Glue and screw through the sides and the transom. The chines and bottom need protection against abrasion, and the outside rubbers combined with the inside cross-members serve to stiffen the bottom. At the chines bend strips

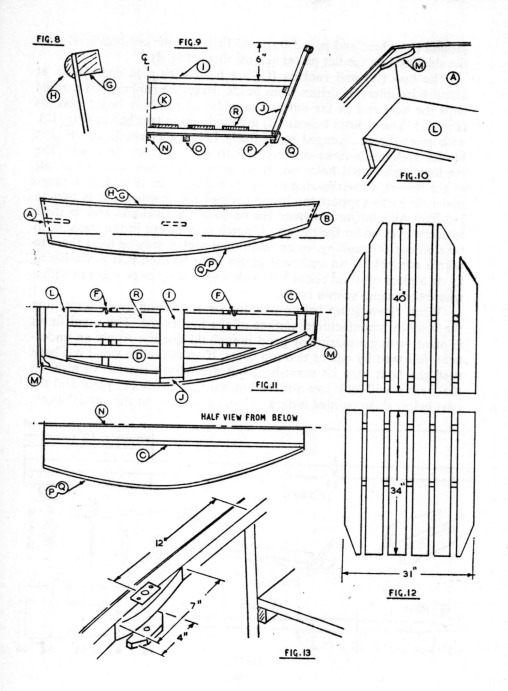

FIG. 8

FIG.9

FIG.10

FIG.11

HALF VIEW FROM BELOW

FIG.12

FIG.13

around (P), glued and nailed through. Plane off the outsides level with the sides and fix the flat pieces against them (Fig. 4).

The keel (N) and rubbers (O) are fixed with glue and screws at about 6 in. intervals driven from inside. Keep the rubbers (O) parallel with the keel and as far out as the width of the bow board permits (Fig. 11). The bottom boards (R) are made up in two halves (Fig. 12), with cross-pieces arranged to fit freely between pieces E and F. Put blocks and turnbuttons on pieces F to hold the boards down. The rowlock plates need holes nearly as thick as the gunwales, 12 in. aft of the thwart, so reinforcing pieces should be fitted (Fig. 13). Arrange under-cleats to support the lower ends of the rowlocks. It is best to put light rope lanyards around the necks of the rowlocks and tie them to screw eyes under the thwart. A notch may be cut in the transom to take an oar for sculling, or an additional socket may be fixed there to take a rowlock. If an outboard motor is to be used it is advisable to fix on a piece of wood about 1 ft. wide and as deep as possible to stiffen where the cramp screws come.

When cleaning up before painting or varnishing avoid scratching the smooth manufactured surface of the hardboard. The usual finish is paint—using a marine or good household quality. Apply an under-coat, followed by one or two top coats. If an attractive wood has been used the boat may be varnished, but use only a marine varnish. In that case it will look smart if the bottom boards are left plain and the part below them painted a dark colour in contrast to the varnishwork.

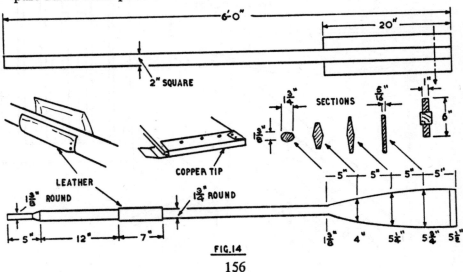

FIG.14

156

Use oars about 6 ft. long, preferably spoon-bladed spruce, although ash may be better for coastal use. These may be bought, but if they are to be made, a straight-bladed type is possible with ordinary tools (Fig. 14). Use a synthetic resin glue to join the parts, then draw the outlines of the blades and cut them out. Mark a centre line around the edge of the blade, and use this as a guide to plane the blade to about $\frac{5}{16}$ in. thick all round with a ridge down the centre. Plane the loom octagonal, then take the corners off and round it with glasspaper. Reduce the size of the grip. Put leather at the point of wear and protect the tip with thin copper, tacked on. Fix a length of rope to each of the bottom knees—and you are ready to launch your craft.

MATERIALS REQUIRED FOR THE DINGHY

All sizes are in inches and widths and thicknesses of wood are finished sizes.

Part	Name	No. Required	Length	Width	Thickness
A	Transom	1	36	15	$\frac{1}{4}$
B	Bow Board	1	18	9	$\frac{1}{4}$
C	Bottom knees	2	12	4	$\frac{1}{2}$
D	Chines	2	87	$\frac{3}{4}$	$\frac{3}{4}$
E	Stiffener	1	40	$\frac{3}{4}$	$\frac{3}{4}$
F	Stiffener	2	36	2	$\frac{1}{2}$
G	Gunwales	2	96	$\frac{3}{4}$	$\frac{3}{4}$
H	Rubbing strip	2	96		$\frac{1}{2}$ round
I	Thwart	1	44	7	$\frac{7}{8}$
J	Thwart supports	2	12	7	$\frac{3}{4}$
K	Thwart support	1	8	4	$\frac{3}{4}$
L	Stern sheets	1	36	7	$\frac{1}{2}$
M	Quarter knees	4	6	3	$\frac{1}{2}$
N	Keel	1	84	$\frac{3}{4}$	$\frac{3}{4}$
O	Rubber	2	84	$\frac{3}{4}$	$\frac{3}{4}$
P	Chine rubbers	2	87	$\frac{3}{4}$	$\frac{3}{4}$
Q	Side rubbers	2	87	$1\frac{1}{4}$	$\frac{1}{2}$
R	Bottom boards	6	35	4	$\frac{1}{8}$
	Bottom boards	6	41	4	$\frac{1}{8}$
	Bottom boards	4	32	$1\frac{1}{2}$	$\frac{1}{8}$

Oil-tempered hardboard:
Bottom—one piece 82 × 40 × $\frac{1}{8}$
Sides—two pieces 96 × 15 × $\frac{1}{8}$

Brass screws, countersunk (figures approx):
1 gross $\frac{5}{8}$ in. × 4 gauge (main construction)
4 doz. $\frac{3}{4}$ in. × 5 gauge (end grain fastenings)
2 doz. 1 in. × 6 gauge (thwarts, knees)

1 doz. 1$\frac{1}{2}$ in. × 6 gauge (thwarts, knees)

Nails (approx):
$\frac{1}{4}$ lb. $\frac{3}{4}$ in. × 17 gauge brass nails (main construction)
$\frac{1}{4}$ lb. 1 in. × 12 gauge copper boat nails (rubber, bottom boards)
Glue: Two packs Aerolite 306 or two 18 oz. cans Cascamite One-shot
Rowlocks: 1 pair 2 in. galvanized, with plates.

COLUMBUS (SALVADOR)

BALBOA (PANAMA)

CORDOBA (NICARAGUA)

DA SOUZA (BRAZIL)

BOLIVAR (COLOMBIA, ECUADOR, VENEZUELA)

PIONEERS

AND

HEROES

A SURPRISINGLY small number of portraits of pioneers and national heroes have appeared on modern coins. Most of those that have appeared come from the American continent.

Salvador honours Columbus on an imposing coin and Panama shows its great discoverer Balboa who, from "a peak in Darien", had the first sight of the Pacific. Nicaragua depicts one of her pioneers, the Spaniard, Cordoba.

Brazil celebrated the fourth anniversary of its colonization by the Portuguese with coins showing Da Souza, its first Governor-General.

The honoured memory of Simon Bolivar is perpetuated on the coins of three of the states he helped to liberate from Spanish rule—Colombia, Ecuador, and Venezuela. Chile has paid tribute to the gallant patriot, Bernardo O'Higgins (of Irish ancestry).

Two immortal Englishmen have appeared on commemorative half-dollars of the U.S.A. Captain James Cook was featured on the coin issued in 1928 to mark the 150th anniversary of the discovery of Hawaii, where he was killed by the natives; while the half-dollar celebrating the 305th anniversary of Roanoake Island, South Carolina, gives a fine portrait of Sir Walter Raleigh, whose landing there in 1584 led to the colonization of Virginia.

Another half-dollar piece commemorates the bicentenary of Daniel Boone, the great scout and frontiersman.

HELLIER

O'HIGGINS (CHILE)

CAPTAIN COOK

SIR WALTER RALEIGH

DANIEL BOONE

HELLIER

CHRISTMAS CROSSWORD

Set by GORDON DOUGLAS

Clues Across

1. Pull it to ensure your party gets a good report (7).
7. It will add glitter to your decorations (6).
8. Describes the carol King (4).
9. Calendar or confection (5).
10. They will control Santa's deer, of course (5).
12. Gee, they're flying south-east—straight into the roasting tin? (5).
14. Rag us about it being sweet (5).
16. One of the Wise Men's gifts (4).
17 Ideal geographical head-gear for a snowman (3-3).
18. P.S. enter—and see what's in the Christmas parcel (7).

Clues Down

2. Christmas flowers (5).
3. Find it in a battery, or end up in it for assault and battery (4).
4. Agree to differ but more than willing (5).
5. You may legally steal something under this at Christmas (9).
6. Ring up for fifteen rounds directly after Christmas (6, 3).
9. Animal watch aboard ship (3).
11. Find a knight in desire (3).
13. Duck down! (5).
14. Severe end of the ship (5).
15. Mince matters in these Christmas sweets (4).

(*Solution on page 192*)

159

BUFFALO COUNTRY

by

S. C. GEORGE

JIM KERSHAW was a "new chum" in Australia, and the air trip from Sydney to his uncle's cattle station in the Northern Territory was an adventure in itself.

"You'll be bang on the fringe of Arnhem Land," the pilot told him. "The one part of Australia where a man can get himself speared by wild 'abos'. Plenty of 'em have never seen a white. Can you ride and shoot?"

"I learned to ride back home when I was eight, and they taught me shooting in the school cadet corps," Jim answered.

"Your uncle's station is near buffalo country. As it's the dry season, you might bag one."

"That's what I'm hoping," said Jim.

Buffalo were a plague in Western Arnhem Land. To keep them down, the administrator could grant landholders a licence to kill a specified

The maddened bull changed direction and charged, head down.

number of male buffalo. A hunting trip, Jim thought, might win him a little more respect at school, where the boys mocked his English accent and his ignorance of Australian ways.

"Your uncle's station is best part of a day's trip by truck from the landing-ground," the pilot observed. "Mighty rough going, too."

"He's sending his head drover to meet me," Jim said. "Larry Radford."

"Larry," the pilot laughed. "Nice fella—when you get to know him."

The last few words sounded slightly ominous, but, after the dust of their landing had settled, Jim was prepared to like the picturesque figure who sauntered towards them from the waiting truck.

He was tall, lean, and loosely-knit; a crimson-tipped cockatoo feather slanted jauntily from the 10-gallon hat that shaded a tanned weather-beaten face. He wore a leather coat, and high-heeled riding-boots over tight gaberdines. He looked about twenty-six, ten years older than Jim, and was annoyed at having had to spend a night in a truck to collect a pale-faced schoolboy.

"Hiya, Dick!" he greeted the pilot laconically.

"How's tricks, Larry? Any buffalo lined up for this young hunter?"

"Kangaroo-rat, maybe," Larry sneered, disdainfully eyeing Jim's shot-gun. "Dungarees and a flannel shirt'll be more use than that city clobber," he threw at Jim, taking his suit case and, with a careless wave of the hand, departing for the battered truck.

Jim felt rebuffed, but decided that Larry would look quite pleasant if he could allow his hard mouth to relax in a smile.

"I have brought proper clothes with me, Mr. Radford," he said diffidently to break the silence.

"Larry Radford. There's no misters round here."

"Phew! It's hot," Jim tried again, as Larry slung his suitcase in the back of the truck.

"What did you expect? Snow?"

"Not so pleasant, after all," Jim thought as, wordlessly, they began to lurch through a region of ghost gums and 25-foot ant-hills.

The sun was high when Larry pulled up. "Get out the tucker-bag," he ordered curtly.

He had started a fire before Jim had taken out the corned meat, damper, johnny cakes, and tea.

"What d'ye think we're gonna drink out of?" he demanded testily as Jim sat down.

Jim returned to the truck, found a couple of tin mugs, a can of water, and a tin grimed with smoke. Larry looked on silently as Jim boiled the water and dribbled tea into the mugs.

"More in mine," he grunted. "Make it black." And after the meal, when Jim had trodden out the fire, he remarked, "We'll have an hour's shut-eye. It's a long drive."

But there was too much to interest Jim—a flying-squirrel performing acrobatics on a eucalyptus tree, a flock of chattering green budgerigars, and then he cried out as an ankle-thick ten-foot python wriggled past.

Instantly wide-awake, Larry was on his feet. He looked contemptuously from the snake to the startled boy.

"Don't you know yet they're harmless?" he snapped, lying down again. "The 'abos' eat 'em."

Jim thought miserably that if the other hands were like Larry he

162

would be glad when the holiday was over. And he was sure that Larry would be too.

But his spirits rose when late in the afternoon they approached a group of wooden buildings where aboriginal and white stockmen were repairing fences. One of the "abos" shaded his eyes against the setting sun, then turned and called, and from some wurlies under a group of graceful ironwood trees a colourful crowd of gins and piccaninnies ran out with cries of welcome. This was the "outback" that Jim had so often imagined.

Appraised of their arrival by the noise, Mr. Kershaw swung himself across a horse and cantered towards them.

"Glad to see you, Jim. Had a good trip?" he asked when Larry had driven off after dumping the suitcase on the shady verandah.

"The trip was all right," Jim said, hesitantly, "but I don't think Larry likes me. As a matter of fact, uncle," he confessed, "it's the same with the chaps at school. I just don't seem to get on with Aussies."

"Maybe Larry and school are connected," Mr. Kershaw said thoughtfully.

"How?"

"There's a Tom Radford in your class, isn't there?"

"Yes, it was he who set the others against me, and I once thought he would be my best friend."

A light flashed in Jim's mind. "Is he . . ."

"Larry's young brother," his uncle nodded. "I expect he's told Larry about what he would call your Pommy ways. Don't worry, though. Larry's a decent sort. He has a chip on his shoulder just now."

"Why take it out on me?" Jim complained.

"I'm putting Larry in charge of the buffalo hunting party this year. I can't go myself. No need for disappointment," he laughed at Jim's crestfallen expression. "I've told Larry you'll be going with him. That's what is biting him, but you'll be all right when he's got to know you."

"He doesn't think much of my gun," Jim said ruefully.

"You'll have to take my ·303 for buffalo. Better practise with it this next week. It's dangerous work, but Larry will keep you out of trouble, and you must promise to obey his orders unquestioningly—whatever they may be."

"Of course. He's the leader."

"Your father suggested I should let you go. There'll be six of you altogether. The hunting is usually done in pairs. Larry will pick your targets and show you the ropes. For instance, you can only kill bulls of three years or older. You must know where to aim, too. A shot on the

163

frontal bone that would kill a cow often makes a bull only shake his head."

"Until Dad read me your letter I didn't know there were wild buffalo in Australia," Jim said.

"You're not the only one. Arnhem Land hasn't been fully explored even yet. Actually, all these wild buffalo spring from a few domestic beasts that were imported from Timor more than a hundred years ago and strayed into the bush. They have increased until they are a nuisance —and a dangerous nuisance, too."

*　　*　　*

During the following week Jim practised hard with the ·303, and did his best to cultivate Larry's friendship. But Larry avoided him, and merely commented sourly about his shooting, that knocking a tin can off a fence was no qualification for spoiling a buffalo hunt. He got on much better with Micky, an aborigine who was to accompany them. Larry's attitude was all that spoilt Jim's enjoyment, for he liked the rest of the team—Sandy, Micky, and Paddy, three full-blooded aborigines, and an old-timer, nicknamed Bonzo, who had an amazing repertoire of songs to which he strummed a mandoline accompaniment.

A solid rubber-tyred wagon carried their supplies, and would be used later for the buffalo hides which, washed and salted, would be carted to Darwin for shipment to Sydney where they would fetch £5 or £6 apiece.

Jim was determined to do nothing foolish which might become known at school through Larry's letters, and so confirm the boys in their poor opinion of him.

"This is the life," Bonzo chuckled as they rode from the homestead. "As free as a frog from feathers."

Jim thought so, too, especially at night round the camp fire when he listened to their yarns or Bonzo strumming:

> *For these are the men of the stations,*
> *Who ride 'neath the Northern Star's light,*
> *Where the saltbush blows and the mulga grows,*
> *And men must be men in the fight.*

He liked being awakened in the morning, too, by screaming parrots, and to lie lazily watching Paddy kick the embers into life and build up the fire, and to listen to the clatter of pots and pans until the "abo" turned his wrinkled face towards them, and the broad nostrils of his flat nose widened as he opened his cavernous mouth and roared, "Day-ay-light. Come an' get it."

Then they would sit up from the campsheets and pull on their riding boots and leggings and leather coats. Half an hour to wash, breakfast, and saddle-up before sun-up.

On the fringe of a swamp Jim saw his first buffalo, a young bull with his little herd of six cows grazing on lush grass in a grove of soft, dark needlewood, spreading coolabahs and delicate olive-green mulga.

"A two-year-old," said Larry. "Let him go." When they pitched camp that day, Jim wandered into the bush and, attracted by a low droning, went further than he had intended. In a clearing he came upon a score of aborigines, their scarred bodies decorated with white feathers and ochre. The noise came from a bull-roarer that one whirled round while the others stamped the ground in a wild dance and shook broad-bladed spears.

Jim recalled the pilot's words: "The one part of Australia where a man can get himself speared by wild abos."

The dance stopped when one of them saw him and pointed. Jim turned and fled to warn the others, spurred on by the uproar behind him. But he had got himself "bushed". Finally, almost exhausted, he ventured to shout. A heavy thudding, like the slow beating of a great drum, quickened his pulse. He had left his rifle behind and was defence-less. The drumming stopped, and an old man kangaroo that had been sounding a warning with his tail loped away through the scrub. Jim shouted again, risking discovery by the aborigines, but it was nearly dark when he glimpsed a painted savage on his trail. The man turned, and then Micky and Larry were hurrying towards him.

"Didn't I tell you not to leave the camp on your own?" Larry shouted. "I'd have got the blame if anything had happened to you."

Jim unwisely explained that he thought he had seen a native war-party.

"Them black-fella come because they know soon plenty of meat," Micky grinned. "They do skinning for us. Make corroboree when you see 'em."

Larry said nothing, but his sneer made Jim suspect that another acceptable piece of news would soon be on its way to his brother.

The second disaster followed on the heels of the first. Bonzo, who had been out with the "abos", rode in excitedly.

"Whips o' fats headin' fer the swamp, Larry," he cried, "an' the ground as hard as a gin's heels."

They galloped after Bonzo with the aborigines trotting in the thick grey dust of their wake. Soon they sighted three separate mobs, about thirty in each, moving in the same direction.

165

"Wait here and watch how we cut out the bulls," Larry ordered Jim. "One sniff of us and they'll be gone. Come on, boys. Micky and I will take the leader."

Impatiently he rode his horse against Jim's to thrust him aside. Jim's horse reared, making him drop his loaded rifle. The resulting explosion scattered the herd. The party spurred after them, but there was small chance of overtaking buffalo travelling at top speed on level ground, and, enveloped as they were in dust, none of trying a long shot.

Larry returned in a fury.

"Give the kid a break, Larry," Bonzo said, appeasingly. "It warn't his fault. You rode into him."

"He shouldn't ha' been in my way," Larry stormed. "Bill Kershaw should ha' known better than saddle us with this Pommy kid."

"I'm sorry," Jim apologized, swallowing the insult.

"Sorry! A lot of good that does, but I'll see it doesn't happen again. You've not done a lick of work since you've been with us," Larry said unjustly. "You can take over the cooking from Paddy, and we'll hope the school cadets taught you how to boil water."

He had promised to obey Larry's orders whatever they might be. Sick at heart, he applied himself to his new duties, for he knew something about field-cooking.

A few mornings later an unusual excitement stirred the camp. Most of the preceding night the tribe that had followed them had been singing and dancing to the boom of the didgeridoo and click of clap-sticks.

"They've found a whacking great herd," Bonzo laughed in reply to Jim's question, "and they're thinking of tonight's feast—humps and tongues and roasted ribs till they burst." Then he whispered, "Micky's finding you a guide, but don't let Larry know."

It would be something he might never see again, and Larry had only forbidden him to leave the camp alone. So, when an aborigine beckoned, he mounted his roan and left the pots and pans behind, and followed the hunters.

The native motioned him to stop in fairly open country, and soon the ground shook, and Jim heard high-pitched yells and the bellowing of cattle. Drama began as the monster herd of 200 buffalo swept through the trees, the men riding magnificently alongside as they attempted to cut out the bulls for a fatal shot. The cows were in headlong panic and the bulls bellowing their rage as they turned from time to time desperately on their pursuers. Larry and Sandy were on one side of the herd, Bonzo and the two remaining black drovers on the other.

Jim pitied the buffalo, but his blood tingled at the furious onrush, the reckless riding, and the skill of the horses trained to wheel swiftly for this particular purpose. Men yelled, beasts roared, and the grey dust swirled about pounding hooves and tossing horns.

Jim found himself riding through the yellow scrub after them, shouting with the rest. In a ten-minutes' run of two or three miles, the hunters picked out and brought down fourteen or fifteen bulls.

But Larry was after the leader, an old bull with sweeping horns who was protected by his cows. With apparent disregard for life and limb, Sandy forced his horse into the stampeding mob and turned them aside, leaving the old bull momentarily uncovered. As Larry swung his horse alongside the maddened bull changed direction and charged, head down. The bullet struck its frontal bone without killing it. The bull staggered and stopped, then turned on its tormentor.

Larry's horse pivoted on its hind-legs to avoid the terrible horns. The bull's flank smashed into the horse. It did not fall, but Larry's rifle was torn from his grip in the surge of beasts around him. There was no time to recover it, for the bull had turned upon him again. Sandy was too busy extricating himself from the herd to see what had happened, and Bonzo and his two men were hidden by the dust at the other side of the herd.

Jim realized Larry's danger. There was a chance that he could over-take him and give him his own gun, but shock from the bull's impact had frightened Larry's horse. With ears back and eyes wild it was no longer under control. Yet it was outpacing the bull, and then, when Larry seemed out of danger, his horse put a foot in a rat-hole and Larry flew over its back.

Barely conscious, he was yet able to stagger up and face the ten feet of muscled fury behind the pointed horns.

Jim glimpsed the desperation in his face, and then, when all seemed hopeless, Jim rose in his stirrups and fired from behind the beast at the base of its skull. Maybe it was a lucky shot that crashed into the bull's brain, but it saved Larry's life. The great beast crumpled, was carried on some yards by the force of its charge, and skidded to a stop less than six feet from the winded man.

The excitement over, reaction set in. Jim slipped from his horse and approached Larry on legs of jelly. Larry's smile was warm at last.

"Nice work, cobber," he said, holding out his hand. Jim, gripping it, knew that from now on everything would be all right.

FISHING: Many ways in many Lands

U.S.A.

ZANZIBAR

ASSAM

Spearing fish by torchlight

ANDAMAN ISLANDS

Bow-and-arrow fishing

"Beel fishing" in flooded fields with open-ended baskets

JAPAN

Trained cormorants do the work for Japanese fishermen

CHINA

Otters fish for Chinese fishermen

Indians netting salmon in Columbia River

PHILIPPINES

U.K.

The sea-gypsies dive overboard to spear fish

Fishing by kite from a lighthouse

HELLIER

CAMP COOKS NEED PRACTICE

by

JACK COX

CAMPING gives boys an opportunity to carry out all manner of exciting, adventurous hikes and explorations, and the chance to learn something about country life. If you spend too much time on cooking food all these wonderful opportunities will be missed, or curtailed, and the whole purpose of camping is then defeated. A boy with little camping experience may often feel that half the time is spent in cooking food and the other half in eating it, or trying to eat it. No wonder he becomes disillusioned, especially if it rains hard.

There are trends in camping, just as in other things. The present trend in Scout camping, for instance, favours a week's camp in August, and a site is selected inland in preference to the overcrowded coast. Yet many unspoiled parts of the coast can still be found; the finest camp sites in Britain are still found on farms near the sea. I would like to see a return to summer camps of two, or even three, weeks' duration. So much more practical work can then be done, including test and badge work, and there is more scope for outdoor fun and trying out new ideas. No part of Britain is more than 80 miles from the sea, and it seems a pity not to make every possible use of that geographical fact. Yet I still meet boys in cities like London, Birmingham and Manchester who have never seen the sea in their lives.

The patrol system is the accepted method of running any good Scout troop or camp, yet it can be overdone. I have visited more than one summer camp where patrols are sited close together in the one field available, with Scouters' tents and a camp-fire circle nearby as well. One sees four or five cooking fires in operation with patrols less than ten yards apart, sometimes even next to each other! This is accepted in a Jamboree, or in the boys' camping fields at Gilwell or other well-established camping centres, but it is not the proper way to use B.-P.'s excellent Patrol system. Ideally the patrols should be well apart—80 to 100 yards—and even out of sight of each other, so that each patrol is truly self-contained.

Cutting Camp Costs

If space prevents this and a troop has to camp in a small field then it may be a better plan to consider central cooking, with one camp kitchen and one patrol on cooking duty for a day at a time, cooking for the whole camp, with a Scouter or Rover to help and supervise. If a spell of bad weather hits a camp this is always the best way to solve cooking problems. Central cooking has many advantages at a time when food prices are high, and travelling such an expensive business. The actual cost of food will be at least 10 per cent lower; some youth leaders have proved to me that it can be 20 per cent less than Patrol cooking; there is less waste of food and fuel, and fewer cooking utensils need be bought. It is simpler to operate grid fires, and altar fires; in wet weather a bucket fire takes some beating especially if it is made from one of the large buckets sold for egg preserving rather than a kitchen pail.

It is never safe to leave a camp unattended these days and if a duty patrol is constantly in camp this hazard can be reduced to a minimum, while the rest of the troop can be out all day on wide games, exploring hikes, swimming and sailing fun, or good turns, such as building a bridge over a stream or a dry gully for a farmer. To a good troop accustomed to week-end Patrol camps at other times the use of central cooking at summer camp will be a novelty and a new experience. Money saved in food preparation and cooking may well enable more time to be spent in camp, and a more adventurous programme planned.

Camp cooks need plenty of practice *in the open air*. It is easy to practise cooking skills at home in a modern kitchen, but that does not get a boy far in the open, when he has to contend with wind and sun and rain. If your troop is fortunate enough to own a headquarters of its own, with a bit of spare land available, why not practise there? An altar fire is always an asset, yet they are often built badly, or even dangerously. The best I have seen, and used, were built on second-hand carpenter's benches or a solid old kitchen table of the refectory type (received gratefully as a Jumble Sale offering!) They can be taken to summer camp over and over again if the rammed clay and earth are removed each time and the table or bench cleaned; alternatively you can build one to suit your own convenience in pioneering style on the six-leg pattern.

A grid fire is a better proposition if the camp site is in an open situation. Again it is best to have the grid tailor-made to your own specification to suit the cooking gear you have. A local garage or forge

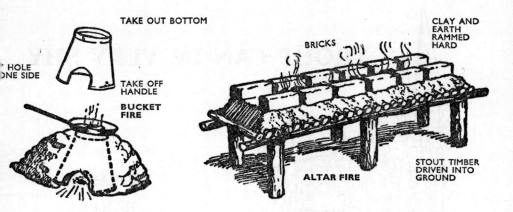

or workshop will make one for you that will give you years of wear;
Messrs. Thos. Black (Greenock) Ltd. sell some excellent folding grids
for smaller camps.

Bricks are Useful

Do not spurn the use of bricks on altar and grid fires. One of the
finest of all outdoor pioneers was David ap Thomas, of Anglesey
origin, who as David Thompson the Welshman, and after whom the
Thompson River is named, mapped and surveyed vast areas of Canada;
he used to make bricks from river clay to line his cooking fires and
preferred these to logs. A bucket fire cooks best if it is surrounded by
earth or clay, with turves as a final touch; a small fire is lit and gradually
built up so that about a third of the space inside is a mass of glowing
red-hot embers. It must be fed regularly but not choked, and each
evening you rake it out like a kitchen boiler. A reflector fire is always
fun, and is the most exciting way to cook fish; you can spread juicy
kippers out and keep them in position with wooden meat skewers or
small mesh wire netting. Mackerel, herring, trout and whole plaice are
also good when cooked this way.

A biscuit-tin oven is worth building. In many parts of North Wales,
for instance, the fields are separated by high, wide earth and stone banks
covered in wild flowers and vegetation in the spring; parts of these earth
walls are often quite bare in August. If your farmer host gives you permission you could build an oven at waist height into one of these banks
with a small, *well-controlled*, hot fire below the biscuit-tin, and a short
stove-pipe to give draught built in at the back. A biscuit-tin would be
much too small for a standing camp; a disused oil cooking stove is better.

TROUT CAN BE VERY SHY

by

NORMAN

BAKER

TROUT fishing is delightful sport; put as much or as little skill and time as you wish into it. Spend moderately. Have fun. Trout are rising in May, but do not rush madly after them. No fish are anxious to hook themselves and trout can be very, very shy. Start by gathering local knowledge. Trout have favourite haunts which can be discovered by patient observation. Prospects vary according to water temperature, its height, light conditions, and the direction and strength of the breeze. About 55 degrees temperature is good and if that comes on a rather dull warm day with a gentle south or south-west wind the outlook is splendid. Ideal conditions are rare, of course. We make the best of whatever comes our way. Local fishing tackle shopkeepers are generally practical anglers and can be relied upon for sound advice especially concerning the right killing fly.

Casts, fly-boxes, and other odds and ends—even a handy 8-foot two-joint fly rod with reel and line to match—are obtainable from the same source, if required. Novices should persuade an old fisherman to show them how fly casting is done. There is no great mystery in this art. In my opinion, it is much easier than swinging a cricket bat straight. Half an hour at the riverside or on a lawn will teach the first essentials of fly casting. After that practice, and a great deal of it, is needed for real efficiency.

Learn Some Simple Knots

When I meet a boy angler I look for neatness and tidy gear. I prefer to see a few well-chosen patterns in various sizes than a large collection of artificial flies; also a properly oiled reel with its line rubbed smooth than a ratchety affair with the mud from last month's outing caked on it. Fishing rods must *never* be put away in a damp cloth case. Rub the inner ferrule with a pencil before assembly and the joints will not stick and refuse to come apart at the end of the day's sport. Hold only the metal ferrules when putting a rod together or taking it down. Hands close together and a quiet firm twist. I have seen stout sea rods as well as delicate fly rods ruined through neglecting these precautions.

Learn the simple Figure-of-Eight knot illustrated for joining your cast loop to the reel line and also the two-circle Turle knot to secure eyed flies. Then you and a hooked trout should not part company on the strike. Hook your fly in the butt ring, run the cast round the

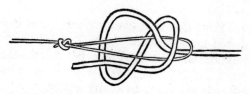

Tying the fly line to the cast with a Figure-of-Eight knot: pass line up through the loop of the cast, then underneath both strands of the loop. Double back on itself leaving a small loop at the side. Bring the end over the top of the cast loop and then up through the small side loop. Draw tight

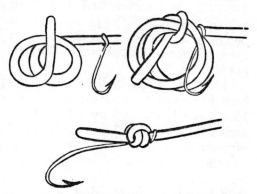

Secure the hook or fly with a Two-Circle Turle knot: thread hook or fly on to cast and slide up out of the way. Make first circle 6 inches from the end and overlay with the second circle. Hold circles with the thumb and forefinger, join the top of the two circles with a slip knot. Push the end of the cast, and then the hook or fly, through the circles and draw all tight round neck of hook

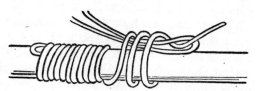

Whipping a rod ring on to the rod: Set the ring in place and lay the end of the whipping twine alongside the foot. Hold in place with the left hand and with the right use the remainder of the twine to bind TIGHTLY round, bury the foot and the end of the twine. After about six turns lay a separate loop of twine on the rod, bury this with four further turns and slip the end of your binding twine through the loop. Pull on the doubled ends of the loop and draw the binding end into the centre of the whipping. Cut off ends

reel and gently wind in all slack. Carry the rod at its point of balance, butt foremost, as you walk to the riverside.

173

Your first cast over a rising trout is supposed to be worth any half-dozen later because the fish should not be aware of your presence or intentions. That may not be strictly true, but there is sound angling sense behind the idea. With it in mind an angler will take proper advantage of any available cover, cast carefully, and try not to disturb his quarry. Whether trout are sought with fly or bait those tactics pay handsomely. It is customary to decry all forms of bait fishing for trout. Without doubt fly and fly only is the most artistic method of catching trout. Anglers increase and trout waters remain about the same. Bait fishing is too deadly for fish stocks to stand the strain. On most fisheries "fly only" is a sound rule, but there are times and places when a truly-spun minnow, a dapped natural insect or even the humble worm is permissible.

Modern trout-spinning outfits serve for a wide variety of angling both in freshwater and the sea. Glass rods 7 feet long are excellent. Handymen build their own with steel tubes from "ex-Govt." wireless aerials for the joints. Fit rings and a cork handle on the upper two joints of an aerial and you have a very practical and well-proved rod at about one-third the price of a factory-made article.

British-made Reels are Best

A bewildering array of threadline reels decorates the trout-spinning department of every tackle shop. Most of them work quite well, but it must be remembered that you get what you pay for as a rule and the cheaper models are not so good as more expensive ones. If a reel of British make is selected there should be no trouble in replacing a damaged part at any future period. Our makers were first in the world with this type of fishing reel and we manufacture the best.

Fill the spool of a threadline reel with 3-lb. or 4-lb. single-strand nylon line and enjoy days with saltwater mackerel in May. Shoals of these hard fighters are wandering inshore looking for brit and other small fry. Any bright trout spinner, a Devon minnow, or the traditional tin or celluloid mackerel spinner are sure killers whether cast out and reeled in as for true spinning or merely trailed behind a slowly moving boat. Feathers are the most popular mackerel lure and when quantity is desired nothing beats them. Ten or a dozen are worked on a handline and I have known a mackerel come up on every hook. Merry sport but not fair angling with rod and line.

Two- or three-feather lures can be used when rod fishing from piers, breakwaters, rocks, or a boat. The lead weighing about half an ounce is looped on the end of the trace and the feather lures stand out on short nylon links like the hooks of a perch paternoster. Work this outfit with a slow sink and draw movement by raising the rod top high and even drawing in a few feet of line through the butt ring by hand. Pollack, school bass, and wrasse may be caught this way. Anglers at Peel, in the Isle of Man, employ a very deadly method for catching large mackerel in the 2-lb.–4-lb. class. Their light spinning outfit ends with a 4-foot trace and single hook about size 6. Bait is a shiny strip of herring or mackerel skin which flashes in a most attractive fashion. It is fished deep down within 2 or 3 feet of the sea bed. Spiral leads are used because they can be readily changed according to the depth and speed of the tide. This idea is worth copying on any breakwater or pier when mackerel are around.

Thousands of freshwater fishermen who depend upon roach, dace, bream, carp, barbel, and other general species for their sport will prepare for the opening day of their season in mid-June. I then renovate an old 11-foot roach rod that has landed many hundredweights of fish. Whippings due for renewal will be cut by laying the knife blade flat along the rod joint to avoid damaging the cane. A set of new upright rings comes on a card from the tackle shop. They are whipped on with fine silk or thread, the whippings being neatly finished off as shown. Thorough washing removes all grease and dirt from the rod and when it is perfectly dry a thin coat of varnish is given. Two or even three coats applied very sparingly are much better than one thick smeary coat. Some anglers put the varnish on with their fingertips instead of a brush. I use both methods and find very little difference provided proper rod varnish is selected and the surface for each coat is perfectly clean. Remember to pay any club subscription when due. Buy a rod licence, if necessary. Then you will have no cause for alarm when the Water Bailiff looms in sight!

THE "C" SHANTY

There was a young lady called Foat,
Who used to sing songs in a boat,
But while singing Top D,
She fell in the sea,
Now Bottom C's her only note!

LEARN SAILING

with

P. W. BLANDFORD

One ship goes east, one ship goes west—
By the self-same wind that blows,
But it is the set of the sails and not the gales,
Which determines the way she goes.

THIS old-time seaman's bit of doggerel shows something of the fascination of sailing, which is still very much alive among the thousands of small-boat sailors. To the landlubber, the idea of using the wind to go in any direction except directly away from it savours rather of magic, yet those in the know can take a boat in any direction they wish up to about 45 degrees of directly towards the wind.

The basic "know-how" of sailing is not difficult to learn, and the beginner can soon begin to get results, yet much of the attraction of the sport is in there always being something more to be learned.

The principles of sailing are the same whatever the boat and rig. Once you can sail a small dinghy you know all the theory needed to sail the largest yacht—although the complexities of rigging will puzzle you. The easiest type of boat to learn in is a knock-about general-purpose dinghy. A racing dinghy is very fine, but its reactions may be too quick for you, and you may find yourself swimming, while still wondering what went wrong. A sturdy dinghy about 10 ft. long with a single lug sail may hardly be a thoroughbred, but it will do almost everything that the racer will—at a more leisurely pace, while you have time to think. If anything goes wrong, the consequences are not likely to be serious.

If nothing was done to give a small boat extra keel surface, it would drift rapidly to leeward when the wind was anything but dead astern. It is not usual to put a fixed keel on a dinghy, because it would be a nuisance in shallow waters. Instead, your boat will have a watertight box above the keel, and in this there will either be a hinged centre-board (A) or a lifting dagger-board (B). Your rudder will also be fairly deep to give additional resistance to blowing sideways through the water. Its blade may be hinged so that it will lift if it strikes the bottom.

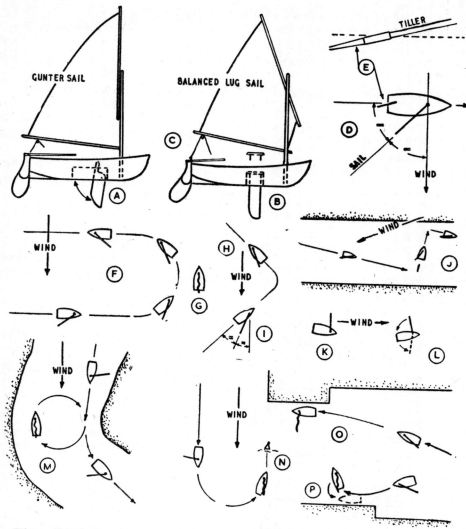

The sail is hoisted by a halliard, which you should make fast within reach, so that you can drop the sail quickly in an emergency. The sail is controlled by a sheet, which you should always hold in your hand. The sheet may come directly from the boom to your hand in the smallest boat, or be given some purchase by leading through blocks as the sail area increases (C).

When sailing single-handed you have the sheet in one hand and the tiller in the other and you sit on the windward side—the side opposite to the sail. As far as possible, position yourself to trim the boat level fore-and-aft. This usually means sitting towards the middle of the boat.

The ideal conditions for a "teach-yourself" sail are a large lake, a steady breeze, and a start from a buoy near the middle of the lake. You may have to manage with very different conditions, but try to have plenty of room and no trees or other obstructions to cause the wind to vary.

It is easier to sail across the wind—called "reaching". The sailor calls a wind on the beam "a soldier's wind", implying that even he could sail in these conditions! To prepare to reach, make sure your centre-board is down and the sheet is free to run out without the end wrapping itself around your feet. If your boat is held to a buoy by your bow painter, it will be swinging like a weather-vane and the sail will be flapping like a flag. Cast off your painter and the boat will sheer one way or the other. Use your rudder to bring the boat across the wind, but do not haul in the sheet.

Your boat will soon gather way, then you can experiment with the angle of your sail. The theoretically best position is with the sail bisecting the angle between the direction of the boat and the direction of the wind (D). However, your sail is not a flat board, and to get the average angle correct you will have to haul the boom in much closer. You may think you are going faster if you haul in the boom too much, because there will be more commotion in the water when the boat heels, but you will not be going as fast as having the sail freer and the boat more upright. If you pay the sheet out, the boat will slow down. Notice, too, another safety device in a properly designed sailing boat. If you let go the tiller, the boat will turn into the wind and stop (E).

When you have sailed as far as you can on a reach, you "go about" to sail back on the opposite course. To do this turn the boat into the wind, by pushing the tiller over gently, to make the boat curve into the wind. The wind will spill out of the sail momentarily as the boat heads directly into the wind. At this point you change sides and hands, ready for when the sail fills again on the other side (F). That is what you should do. Probably, the first time, you will push the tiller over hard so that the rudder blade acts as a brake and you will finish up "in irons" (G)—pointing into the wind, with no way on the boat and inability to complete the manoeuvre.

178

After reaching a few times, try hauling in the boom closer, so that the boat points at an angle towards the wind. The average angle of the sail should still bisect the angle between boat and wind direction (I), which means that the boom will be well over the quarter. A racer will go much closer than a knockabout craft. It is always possible to make the boat appear to point much nearer the wind than it is actually sailing. If you check on marks ashore, you will find that in these circumstances your actual course includes a lot of leeway. The skill in sailing "close-hauled" is in getting the last little bit of progress to windward.

If you wish to make for a point to windward, you must get there by "tacking"—sailing a zig-zag course close-hauled in alternate directions (H). How long you make each "board" depends on your sea room. In a river, with the wind diagonally, you may have to make long and short boards to get where you wish—the shorter boards being little better than straight across the river (J).

Sailing away from the wind is called "running", and the reason it is not so easy as might be expected is that you have less control that way. When reaching or tacking you can always stop by turning into the wind, but when running you may not have room to turn about. It is difficult even to stop by lowering the sail, as the wind fills it until it is stowed. There is also the risk of a "gybe".

To sail with the wind aft, the sheet is paid out until the sail is almost against the standing rigging. When the wind is to one side, the sail is hauled in slightly (K), but with the wind aft, it goes out to a right-angle. In this position there is a risk of the sail being caught aback if the wind changes or you have to follow a bend in the river. Suddenly, the boom will lift and the sail will blow over to the other side (L). This is a "gybe", and the sudden fast swing can do some damage. If you are caught unawares, the boat may capsize. In light airs a controlled gybe is permissible, but it is a manoeuvre that is best avoided. Quite often it is possible to arrange things so that you get where you want to with the wind a few degress away from dead astern.

When you are sailing with the wind astern in a winding river, there are occasions when its meanderings may bring the wind to the wrong side of the sail and you will gybe. If the wind is light and you know the gybe is coming, this does not matter, but if you do not want to gybe it is possible to go about and sail in a tight circle to get the sail on the other side (M). By turning into the wind, the boom crosses over when the sail is flapping empty of air and there is no risk. Providing you have enough way on the boat and there is room for the manoeuvre, this is no more difficult than going about to windward, and is the seamanlike way of dealing with the problem.

Coming alongside or approaching a buoy at the end of a trip is sometimes difficult, particularly when you do not know your boat very well. As far as possible, arrange to bring your boat up into the wind at the end of the trip. In this way you spill the air from the sail and stop the boat. If you have to pick up a buoy, you get downwind of it and sail close-hauled up to it, until you judge that you can spill the wind from the sail and get there merely by the way still on the boat (N). If you are alone and have time, drop the sail before getting forward to grab the buoy.

To come alongside a bank which the wind is blowing off, sail up to it in the direction which allows you to sail nearest to the wind, then gradually slow the boat by easing the sheet, until the sail flaps loosely as your destination is reached (O).

Coming alongside a bank downwind is more difficult. In anything but very light airs the only safe way is to reach along it slowly, then turn up into the wind and drop the sail, so that you either drift or paddle back (P).

Those are all the basic points of sailing technique—the rest is mainly a matter of practice.

In your boat you are concerned with two main problems—the sails, which receive the effect of moving air, and the hull, which is surrounded and supported by water. These combine into the problem of getting the maximum forward motion out of the hull from the effect of the wind on the sails.

The shape of the hull is arranged so that it has the minimum resistance in the direction you want it to go and the maximum resistance to making leeway. If you consider the underwater side view of the hull, you can see that there must be some point about which all the sideways forces on the hull balance. This is called the "centre of lateral resistance". The vertical line on which this comes can be found by balancing a card profile of the underwater section on a knife (Q)— or by involved mathematics if you are that way inclined!

Similarly, with the sails there is a point of balance on which all the forces could be assumed to act. This is called the "centre of effort". It can be found geometrically when the sails are in line with the boat, but there is not much point in this, as they are never there when sailing, except that it has been proved that the best position for the point then

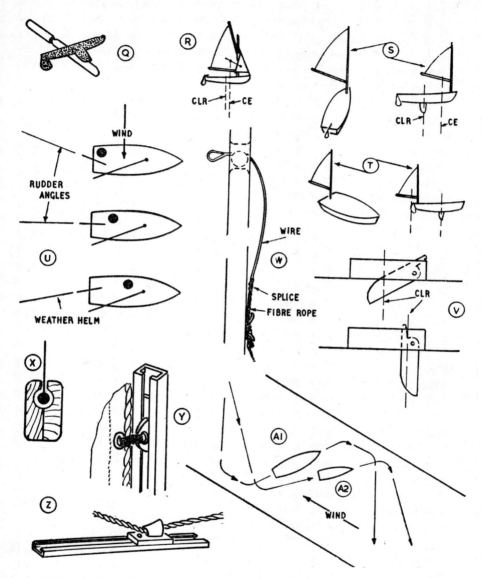

is just forward of the "c.l.r." (R). When sailing "c.e." moves aft of "c.l.r." Where they actually are then is a mystery.

Imagine a boat in which the "c.e." was right up in the bows. No matter what you tried to do, the boat would only sail away from the wind (S). If the boat was rigged at the other extreme, with the wind power aft, it would only turn into the wind and probably sail backwards (T). In a properly balanced boat under way, "c.e." should be slightly aft of "c.l.r." giving a tendency to turn up into the wind—the safety factor, called weather helm.

The "c.e." can only be varied by altering the size of sails. You may reef or change foresails under way, but otherwise you cannot do much about this. However, in a small boat, the location of you and your crew can have a lot of effect on the position of the "c.l.r.". If you are both aft, the stern is deeper and "c.l.r." will come well aft of the "c.e." giving unwanted lee helm, or a tendency to run off the wind. Experiment from this position in a light breeze. Move your weight forward while reaching or sailing close-hauled and notice how the angle of the tiller reduces to keep the same course and eventually moves to a slight angle the other way to give the desirable slight weather helm (U). When there are two of you, the helmsman may stay within reasonable distance of the tiller, while his crew moves forward to give the correct fore-and-aft trim.

Besides the fore-and-aft trim you have to use your weight to trim the boat laterally. There may be plenty of fun in sailing with one gunwale almost under, but the boat will go faster if it is near upright. If yours is a lively craft you will be moving inboard and outboard frequently as the strength of the wind alters—all the time remembering your fore-and-aft positions to maintain the slight weather helm which indicates correct trim. A heavy crew is an advantage as his weight has more effect—a point worth remembering if you want to take the helm when sailing with your father!

Normally, the centre-board or dagger plate is left right down. If you decide to raise it partly because of shallows, the up-and-down motion of the dagger plate has little effect on trim, but you will have to allow for the shifting aft of "c.l.r." as the swinging centre-board comes up (V). That is why record-breaking catamarans have dagger boards instead of what are generally considered superior centre-boards.

Your rudder blade accounts for a lot of underwater area. If it is a hinged one, make sure it stays down. If the shock-cord or spring is weak, it may rise at speed, and you may find yourself sailing the wrong way in a boat that does not respond to its helm.

In recent years sail design has advanced considerably, mostly because of aerodynamic research concerned with problems of flight.

182

A sail going to windward is similar in its action to an aircraft wing in flight. That is why the tall and narrow Bermudan sail has been developed, to give the long leading edge which aircraft design has proved best. A tall sail on a slim mast is more efficient and faster than the shorter more utility rigs. The thickness of the mast upsets the airflow to a certain extent. The fore-sail does not have this handicap, so if it is properly set it can be a big help in clawing to windward. The fitting of your sails has considerable effect on the efficiency of your boat and the enthusiast can profitably spend quite a time on setting everything up to his liking.

Some people would have the mast set up as tightly as possible, but others argue that it makes no real difference. However, for tightness fine strong wire rigging has been developed and the advantage of this in any case is in lessening windage, so whether you gain by tightening or not, thin rigging wire should be an advantage.

Sails should be set up tight. Fibre rope expands and contracts with its moisture content, so it is worth while using flexible wire for the part of a halliard which takes the load of a hoisted sail. If its tail is fibre, there is no difficulty about stowing it (W). The sail should be hauled tight along its spars, but not excessively, otherwise there will be creases and distortion. Make sure any lacing is even. Modern sails either have the bolt rope in a groove (X) or there is a track (Y). This allows a more even tension and a better air flow over the sail near the mast. It is not difficult to convert some boats from lacing to track.

Modern foresails or jibs overlap the main sail. This gives a better air flow over the back of the main sail, but it does introduce the problem of sheeting. For ideal setting the angle of the jib sheet has to be changed between the flattened sail when close-hauled and the greater curve of running. To allow this there can be a sliding fairlead on a track on each gunwale (Z).

When you have the sails set to your satisfaction, improvements in sailing will come with experience. As you get to know your boat you will get more out of it. When a light racing boat goes about in tacking to windward, it almost spins on the spot. It points very close to the wind and turns quickly (A2). The heavier utility boat is more sedate, but once it is moving it carries its way much longer. This can be taken advantage of in tacking in a narrow waterway. Instead of trying to point too high, effort is concentrated on getting the boat moving, then the way is used to carry the boat around in a large sweep, so that most of the actual progress is achieved between tacks (A1).

BUDGERIGARS—
for pleasure and profit

by ERIC LEYLAND

IF you want a hobby which never loses its interest, requires little money to start, and can show a profit at the end of every year, then take up budgerigar breeding. Maybe you think it must cost quite a lot to start this hobby? It can if you start buying ready-made equipment at fancy prices, but not if you make your own. This is quite easy and very cheap. You need two cages (one as a breeding-cage for the parent birds and one as a nursery for the chicks), a nest-box, one or two nest con-caves and, of course, a pair of birds. Equipment and birds should not cost more than £3. You can recover this amount in your first breeding season.

First you must make the two cages. The sketch shows you exactly how to make the breeding-cage. The nursery cage can be similar except that no hole is bored as entrance to the nest-box and no nest-box is provided. Use hardboard for the back, the two ends, the top, and the bottom. Budgerigars should always be kept in this sort of cage, and never in an open wire cage, which can be very draughty. Hardboard is

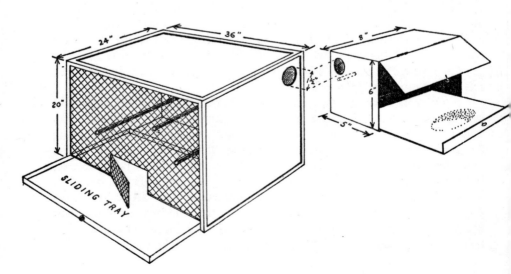

also used for the sliding tray at the bottom, which makes for easy cleaning. Wire-netting of $\frac{1}{2}$-in. mesh, not bigger, forms the front of each cage; a door is made to hinge either in the front, as shown, or if you prefer in one of the solid ends. Use $\frac{1}{2}$-in. battening as the framework for the hardboard.

The breeding-cage for a single pair of birds should measure 36 in. long, 24 in. deep and 20 in. high. The nursery cage can be smaller although in the same proportions, but it is as well to make it the same size. In the breeding-cage, bore a hole $1\frac{1}{2}$ in. diameter as shown in the sketch. Then make the nest-box as shown in the sketch, using $\frac{1}{4}$-in. or $\frac{1}{2}$-in. thick ply for the job, tacking sides and ends together, but hinging the flap opening. This extends only three-quarters of the way down the box. Tack a strip of wood to the side of the nest depression to fill in the gap. Bore another hole $1\frac{1}{2}$ in. in diameter in one end of the box so that when the box is tacked to the end of the cage the two holes coincide. This is the female budgerigar's entrance.

The small perch, about 2 in. long and $\frac{1}{2}$ in. thick, is not fixed under the holes until after the box is tacked to the end of the breeding-cage. Use a headless nail for the job and also to fix the three perches in the cage itself to the hardboard back. The front of each perch will fix easily in the wire-netting. They should all be of wooden dowelling $\frac{1}{2}$ in. thick. Fix similar perches in the nursery cage.

Wooden "Nests"

Budgerigars lay their eggs in the wooden depression. No nesting material should be supplied. If you wish you can buy "concaves", as budgerigar nests are called, at any pet shop, but it is easy to make a depression in the floor of the cage with a chisel as shown. The dimensions of the box are given but these can be altered to suit the size of the concave. A wire hook can be used to fasten the hinged flap into position. Seed, water, and grit containers can be ordinary saucers or anything else convenient. Make a point of supplying grit in a container and do not rely on the small amount of grit in the sand which you use for covering the bottom tray of each cage.

All this equipment should not cost you more than 30s. if you make it yourself. A pair of one-year-old birds, ready for breeding, as they are at about this age, should also cost 30s. the pair. Look in your local paper for advertisements inserted by small local breeders or ask your local pet shop for addresses. Breeders will charge about 15s. each for birds and give you some good advice as well. If you buy direct from a pet shop, try and take an adult with you who knows a good bird when he sees one. A young bird should look sleek and fresh in plumage and colour. Choose a blue and a green. Their chicks will then be varied, green and blue too, but the blue will be a nice deep shade, whereas two blues, although they will produce all blues, also produce indifferent shades. In normal colours the cock will carry a blue pad above the beak, known as the cere; the hen has a brown or fawn cere, unless, as sometimes happens in a blue, the hen's cere is white.

The breeding season starts about April 1 and ends on September 1 for those without special artificial heating and without experience. If you start the hobby out of season, place the two birds in the cage, block up the nest-box hole and let them grow used to each other. Unblock the hole on April 1. If you start during the season, block up the hole for about a fortnight after you get the birds together. You have very little else to do except feed the birds, using a mixture of half canary seed and half white millet, providing fresh water, grit, green-stuff (the best being chickweed in season, and lettuce, watercress or other kitchen garden greens out of season), plus cuttlefish, for them to nibble at, or an iodized niblet. During the breeding season increase the amount of greenstuff and change it every day.

When the hen begins to enter the nest-box you will know that the first egg will soon be laid. Open the box flap every day. When the first egg appears make a note of the date. The second will be laid on the third day, the third on the fifth and so on. Chicks will also hatch out each alternate day. Incubation period is eighteen days, but I allow twenty because the hen often doesn't sit on the first egg and a margin should be allowed. If you note the date on which each egg is laid, then at the end you will know that an unhatched egg is infertile and you can take it away, after the full twenty days have elapsed.

Don't fuss the birds. They know exactly what to do and will feed and rear the chicks without any help from you. No special food is necessary for the chicks. The parents take seed into the crop, half-digest it and then regurgitate to feed the chicks. Don't handle the eggs, but you can and must handle the chicks. Examine them each day. Take away any chick that may have died. Clean the concave or depression every third day at least after the chicks have hatched. The parent birds will not mind your taking chicks out while you clean up; better still, replace the dirty concave with a spare clean one. Replace the chicks carefully and do not let them get cold while they are out of the box.

After about thirty days the chicks will leave the box of their own accord. They will learn to feed themselves in about a week or ten days. The parents will go to nest again. Never allow the chicks of the first round to be in the box or cage when those of the second round are due to be hatched. If you do the female may well kill the first batch! Allow two or at the most three nests in a season. Any nest which does not hatch at all does not count. It is the feeding of the chicks which takes it out of the hen, and cock, who will feed the hen and the chicks as well if necessary. Block up the nest-hole on September 1. If eggs are laid after this, on the floor of the cage, merely destroy them.

Chicks can be sold for about 10s. to 15s. each when they are two months old. If you breed ten in a season, then you will make a good profit, even allowing for capital outlay. The cost of feeding a bird is about a penny a week, or less if you have a large number. If you plan to increase your activities, make more cages during the winter, or even an outdoor aviary in the garden, which again can be made very cheaply. There are plenty of books on the market to tell you all about aviaries and also about many finer points, such as breeding to produce certain colours and so on. But you do not need to be an expert to start successful budgerigar breeding.

STUNTS AND IDEAS
FOR THE CLUBROOM

SCOUTS are always seeking *good* games. Here are some proved good ones for winter indoor meetings. A game to improve "smartness off the mark" is **"First!"** The game leader stands in some central position and says a whole host of things beginning with "First . . .". "First Scout to touch oak!" "First off the floor!" "First in complete Scout uniform at the alert!" "First Scout to tie a bowline!" and so on. The game leader can vary his commands by signalling them or writing them in the troop code.

The **Magic Circle** is a firm favourite. The game leader draws a circle about a yard in diameter on the troop-room floor in chalk. The circle should not be in any central position or a corner. The patrols are given a brief thirty seconds to memorize the position of the circle. Then lights are snapped out. Scouts creep forward from one end of the room and have to halt when they think they are in the circle. Lights are put on again after one minute and Scouts must freeze where they are. The patrol with the greatest number of Scouts in or near the circle wins. This game will test a boy's sense of direction, also an important and little-known sense which we call "fixation".

Here's a game that is packed with Scout training. Make a number of obstacles with logs, chairs, ropes, and so on. Now let each patrol have a "victim". On the word "go" each member of the patrol (if he is physically able to do so) has to carry in turn the "victim", using the fireman's lift, to the opposite end of the troop-room and back over all obstacles. As well as being an exciting patrol race, it teaches a boy how to carry an insensible person over obstacles in, say, a smoke-filled room, an emergency that might have to be faced in any kind of building.

If we think our patrols are good at **Map Reading,** let's try this quick-thinking game. Have a one-inch map of the district mounted on a piece of soft wood. Then stand about 6 feet away and throw a dart at the map-board. (If we don't want to mark it too much, then we can use a piece of soft, sticky wax or plasticine.) As the dart (or wax) hits the board say: "There's a fire at that point! Where's the nearest fire alarm? Nearest doctor? Nearest hospital?" Other versions are: "There's been an accident there," or "A stranger wants to get to the nearest railway station from that point. What's his quickest route?" We can make this perfectly grand game as original as we like, based entirely on our own district. It is one of the best training games.

Impromptu **Ice Hockey** is a real winner. Have two simple goals at either end of the troop-room. The two teams (five-a-side) can be of members of one patrol. In fact an inter-patrol tournament is easy to arrange. The "chuck" is a piece of polished hardwood about 3 inches square and 1 inch thick. Each Scout has a short stout stick about 2 feet long. (*Don't use Scout staffs for this game.*) Goals are scored as in ice hockey and the same rules can be used. The referee should be *very strict* on ankle-tapping, lifting the stick above shoulder height and any kind of rough play. This is a skilful, fast indoor game.

Try also playing it with the smallest size soccer ball, or a junior-size rugger ball, instead of the chuck. The sticks can be replaced by real cut-down hockey sticks if you are as lucky as we were, for we found a hockey club disbanding!

Scouts who are keen campers may well think about **Winter Camping.** It is a tough, hardening experience, even in a mild winter, and is a *Senior* Scout and Rover Scout activity. Many keen campers among young Scouts are eager to try the idea. But we do *not* recommend it for young Scouts in the twelve to fifteen age group, nor would any winter camper of real experience.

Even Senior Scouts have to adopt special technique! Winter Camping should only be done by Senior Scouts in small parties under expert adult leadership. B.-P. always said: "A Scout is not a fool." So we say: "No one but a very experienced camper would go camping in winter. At your age you just haven't got the experience. Wait for April and May and we'll get down to camping proper."

Keen campers can do something, however, at this time of the year. Let's go through our list of patrol camp sites near home, those sites which are within, say, ten or fifteen miles of your home and which are used for week-end patrol camping during the spring and summer.

Good campers always try to see their camp sites under the worst possible weather conditions. This enables them to study drainage, prevailing winds and local weather lore. Then if we had a spell of heavy rain or bad weather during summer camp we would be prepared.

So get your patrol out on bikes on winter week-ends. Go and see all the local camp sites. They look very different now compared to the summer months. Make brief reports with a map; and if one troop shares the sites with other patrols and troops, as often happens, let them have copies. This will all help to build up the troop's camping experience. We cannot spend too much time exploring and studying camp sites.

But if the seniors are keen to try camping in February we are going to make the most of that interest in the next troop meeting. Let's imagine that we are stranded in the backwoods, in the wilderness of the mountains of British Columbia, in the Far West of Canada, if we want a real-life setting. Let each patrol, in its own den or corner, make up the contents of an "emergency kit" for an individual or lone camper under such conditions.

To get the atmosphere right give each patrol a flat tin, with a lid, about 6 inches by 4 inches by 1 inch. A tobacconist will no doubt be able to give you three identical lidded tins very easily. Give no clues at all as to what we as Patrol Leaders would put in such a kit. You may have the quietest night you've had for a long time!

When this game was first played patrols produced lists containing Elastoplast dressings, nylon fishing-line, fishhooks, waterproof matches, compass, powerful magnifying-glass, steel mirror that could also act as a signalling helio if necessary, razor-blades, small supply of highly concentrated foods such as Nescafé, soup concentrate or dehydrated meat, miniature first-aid kit, needles, thread, pins, small powerful magnet, map on silk not paper, small hank of tough light twine, scissors, and a sharpening-stone for a sheath-knife.

Let the troop discuss and criticize all selections at length and let the boys decide which patrol put up the best show. There may be debatable points, such as that powerful small magnet in a steel box with a compass! When the kit has been discussed at length, put forward a Patrol Leader's point of view: if a man is in difficult country alone he may need an immediate food supply and the opportunity to catch food more than anything else. Dehydrated food, and a fishing-line and hooks, yes! He will have to make a fire for cooking the fish or game he catches. The waterproof matches and the magnifying-glass for lighting bone-dry tinder, yes! And he needs a fire at night to keep bears and moose and mountain lynx away. Yes! What animals *are* there in British Columbia? Do they include bear, moose, and lynx? Do they attack men?

190

SOLUTIONS

SUPERINTENDENT SLADE'S CASE-BOOK

THE SHREWD BANKER (*pages 26–27*)

The caller who claimed to be the Stephen Spence of the telephone message had stated definitely that the cheque had been made out just before Mr. Martin phoned the bank manager. If that were the case, Henry Martin would scarcely have made the mistake of dating it the previous day, especially as the 10th was a Sunday and his mind was very much on a Monday business deal.

PHOTO QUIZ (*See Plate 2, opposite page 48*)

The career—Police. *Left to right, top to bottom:* 1. Handcuffs; 2. Torch; 3. Chain on Cape; 4. Truncheon; 5. Notebook; 6. Police-Sergeant's stripes.

THE KNIGHT'S GAME (*Page 52*)

1st Row:	1	24	27	30	11	22	35	32
2nd Row:	26	29	12	23	34	31	10	21
3rd Row:	13	2	25	28	49	58	33	36
4th Row:	64	47	60	57	62	55	20	9
5th Row:	3	14	63	48	59	50	37	54
6th Row:	44	41	46	61	56	53	8	19
7th Row:	15	4	43	40	17	6	51	38
8th Row:	42	45	16	5	52	39	18	7

SPORTS QUIZ (*page 63*)

1. West Bromwich Albion (soccer). 2. Salford (Rugby League). 3. Swansea Town (soccer). 4. Bridgend (Rugby Union). 5. Blackheath (Rugby Union). 6. Watford (soccer). 7. Oldham (Rugby League). 8. Preston North End (soccer). 9. Northampton (Rugby Union). 10. Wasps (Rugby Union). 11. Millwall (soccer). 12. Manchester University (soccer, Rugby Union). 13. Moseley (Rugby Union). 14. Cambridge University (Rugby Union). 15. Bournemouth (soccer). 16. Edinburgh Academical (Rugby Union, scene of the first Rugby International in Scotland v. England 1871.)

Note that both Blackheath and Wasps are called "Football Clubs" and not "Rugby Football Clubs". This is because both were founded before the formation of the Rugby Union in 1871.

TRAINSPOTTERS' CROSSWORD (*page 77*)

Across: 1. Signal. 4. Clear. 7. Toe. 8. Uncouple. 9. Return fare. 11. Sir. 12. Awe. 15. Sudden stop. 16. Steamers. 17. All. 18. Canon. 19. Points.
Down: 1. Saturday. 2. Great Western. 3. Lining. 4. Choral. 5. Express train. 6. Rue. 10. Grapples. 13. Odd man. 14. Tear up. 16. Sac.

CHRISTMAS CROSSWORD (*page 159*)

Across: 1. Cracker. 7. Tinsel. 8. Good. 9. Dates. 10. Reins. 12. Geese. 14. Sugar. 16. Gold. 17. Ice-cap. 18. Present.
Down: 2. Roses. 3. Cell. 4. Eager. 5. Mistletoe. 6. Boxing Day. 9. Dog. 11. Sir. 13. Eider. 14. Stern. 15. Pies.

SPOT THE VINTAGE MAKES (*pages 82–83*)

1. Morris Cowley Saloon 1924
2. Riley Brooklands 1930
3. Invicta 4½ Litre 1930
4. Trojan 10 H.P. 1924
5. Armstrong Siddeley 1922
6. Lagonda 11.9 H.P. 1922
7. Tamplin Cycle Car 1921
8. Austin 7 H.P. 1922
9. Hillman "Speed Model" 1921
10. Rolls Royce Phantom II 1930
11. Morgan "Aero" 1928
12. Bentley 4½ Litre 1928

HIDDEN SPORTS (*page 84*)

1. Boxing (Box-sing); 2. Show-Jumping; 3. Rugby (Rug-bee); 4. Water-Polo (Marco Polo); 5. Cricket (Crick-Et*na*); 6. Tennis (Ten is); 7. Soccer (Sock-cur); 8. All-in Wrestling (All-in-rest-ling); 9. Hundred-Yards Sprint; 10. Baseball; 11. Archery (Ah!-cherry); 12. Badminton (Bad Minton).

COUNTRIES PUZZLE (*page 99*)

The correct solution was: Guatemala, Bulgaria, Germany, Indonesia, France, Spain, Switzerland, Argentina.

TEN-MINUTE MYSTERY (*page 109*)

Stevens was plainly lying, and with the purpose of throwing suspicion on a fictitious cyclist. If such a club cyclist—not in mac!—rode both up and down the lane while the surface was wet he would have left *four* sets of discernible tracks. Only two were found, suggesting someone who habitually kept to the left when *leaving* the Grange. These could have been made by Stevens when he left. His tyres were probably well worn as revealed by the need to mend a puncture. That was plainly why he had since fitted new ones, to attempt to fool the police. But he hadn't been smart enough to make a double set of tracks.

CHESS PROBLEMS (*page 133*)

No. 1

White wins by 1, R × P, B–B1 (if 1 ... P × R; 2, Q–Kt4 (ch), Kt–Kt3; 3, B–K6; and if 1...P × B; 2, Q–Kt4 ch, Q–Kt2; 3, B–K6 ch; Kt × B; 4, Q × Kt ch, etc.); 2, B × B, P × R (if 2...R × B; 3 B–K5, etc.); 3, Q–Kt4 ch, K–R2; 4, B–Q4, Q–Kt1 5, B–B5 ch, Kt–Kt3; 6, P–KR4, etc.

No. 2

Black plays 1 ... R–R5, and after 2, Q–Kt2 the continuation is 2 ... Kt × B; 3, R × Kt, Q–B4; 4, R × P (best), Q × BP ch; 5, Q–K2, Q × Q ch; 6, K × Q, R × P ch; 7, K–K3, K–Kt3, and Black has won a Pawn and has the better position.

No. 3

1, Kt–R7, winning a piece. If 1 ... B–Q2; 2, P × Kt; if 1 ... R × Kt; 2, R × B ch, Kt–B1; 3, Q–Kt6, etc.; and if 1 ... Kt–B2; 2, Kt × B, R × Kt; 3, Q × KtP, etc.

No. 4

1, P–K5, P–Kt4; 2, Q–R5, P × P; 3, Kt × P, R–KR2; 4, Kt–Kt4, R(K1)–K2; 5, Q–Kt6 (ch), R(K2)–K Kt 2; 6, Kt–B6 (ch), K–R1; 7, Kt × R and wins.